adored

D1427891

By Cecily von Ziegesar

IT GIRL novels
The It Girl
Notorious
Reckless
Unforgettable
Lucky
Tempted
Infamous
Adored

GOSSIP GIRL prequel
It Had To Be You

GOSSIP GIRL THE CARLYLES
GOSSIP GIRL THE CARLYLES:
You Just Can't Get Enough
GOSSIP GIRL THE CARLYLES:
Take A Chance On Me

adored

created by
Cecily von Ziegesar

headline

Copyright © 2009 Alloy Entertainment

The right of Alloy Entertainment to be identified as the Author of
the Work has been asserted by them in accordance with the
Copyright, Designs and Patents Act 1988.

First published in 2009 by
Little, Brown and Company, USA

First published in paperback in Great Britain in 2009 by
HEADLINE PUBLISHING GROUP

2

Apart from any use permitted under UK copyright law, this publication may
only be reproduced, stored, or transmitted, in any form, or by any means,
with prior permission in writing of the publishers or, in the case of
reprographic production, in accordance with the terms of licences
issued by the Copyright Licensing Agency.

All characters in this publication are fictitious and any resemblance
to real persons, living or dead, is purely coincidental.

Produced by Alloy Entertainment,
151 West 26th Street, New York, NY 10001

Cataloguing in Publication Data is available from the British Library

ISBN 978 0 7553 4672 1

Typeset in Garamond 3 by Palimpsest Book Production Limited,
Grangemouth, Stirlingshire

Printed in the UK by
CPI Mackays, Chatham ME5 8TD

Headline's policy is to use papers that are
natural, renewable and recyclable products and made from
wood grown in sustainable forests. The logging and manufacturing processes
are expected to conform to the environmental regulations
of the country of origin.

HEADLINE PUBLISHING GROUP
An Hachette UK Company
338 Euston Road
London NW1 3BH

www.headline.co.uk
www.hachette.co.uk

I was adored once, too.

William Shakespeare, *Twelfth Night*

A WAVERLY OWL DOES NOT DISAPPOINT HER ADMIRERS.

Jenny Humphrey leaned against a dark oak window frame in Dumbarton 303 on the Tuesday evening after Thanksgiving break. She stared out at the Waverly campus, blanketed in snow and bathed in the yellowy orange glow of the gaslit lamps that lined the walkways. Clumps of students bundled in cashmere scarves and long wool coats trundled across the quad to the dining hall, occasionally pausing to pack a few snowballs. A lone figure was rolling a snowman out in the middle of the smooth, white lawn.

'Are you guys ready for dinner yet?' Jenny asked over her shoulder. Her stomach rumbled, reminding her that she'd skipped lunch to finish her paper on *The Portrait of a Lady* and was now completely famished.

Unfortunately, her roommate, Callie Vernon, was still in

the process of unpacking the overstuffed Louis Vuitton suit-case that had been flung across their spare bed since she'd returned from her shopping-filled Thanksgiving break in Atlanta. The process was taking twice as long as it should have, since Callie insisted upon holding up each new garment for the admiration of Jenny and Tinsley Carmichael.

'. . . and this is from this tiny boutique in downtown Atlanta.' Callie waved a flimsy red Milly silk tank dress with the tags still on it in front of Tinsley's half-closed eyes, ignoring Jenny's dinner plea.

Tinsley lay on her back on Callie's unmade bed, her dark, almost black hair tumbling off the edge. She raised her violet-colored eyes from the well-thumbed copy of Italian *Vogue* she was flipping through. 'A little racy for the governor's taste.'

Callie tossed her wavy strawberry blond hair over her shoulder and grabbed a hanger from her closet. 'She felt so terrible about the whole *Maine incident* that she didn't say no to anything.'

Jenny giggled and drew a small heart in the condensation that covered the windowpane. Callie's mother, the governor of Georgia, had been under the mistaken impression that Callie had some sort of drug problem, and the month before had sent her off to a boot-camp rehab facility in the middle of nowhere, where she'd almost frozen to death in the snow. Until, that is, her boyfriend, Easy Walsh, came to rescue her – and then subsequently got expelled by Dean Marymount for leaving campus and violating his probation.

It was still shocking to Jenny that Callie had broken up with Easy over Thanksgiving break. This was after he'd managed to escape from the West Virginia military school where his father had sent him post-expulsion, and waited for her atop the Empire State Building. It was so romantic, and with such a sad ending, that it broke Jenny's heart. She knew it was painful for Callie, who, despite exuding an aura of self-assured sophistication, had an almost childlike need for constant affection from her boyfriend. Easy's banishment to military school, where he wasn't allowed phone calls or e-mail, had been too much for Callie. Even though it had only been a few weeks, Callie couldn't handle the long distance, the lack of communication, the uncertainty.

Jenny's stomach let out a giant gurgle. She pressed her hands to her belly, pretending to straighten her black cotton Gap turtleneck. Next to Callie and Tinsley in their expensive designer clothes, it was hard not to feel like a reject from the Filene's Basement bargain bin. 'Guys, I've got to get to dinner before I pass out.'

'Can you just wait like three minutes?' Callie stared at Jenny through her blondish eyelashes, which she usually covered with mascara. She had on a baby blue ruffle-front Juicy Couture blouse and a flowered Robert Rodriguez high-waisted skirt that cost more than a first-class plane ticket. 'I'm almost done.'

Tinsley stuffed a hand in the pocket of her black, slim-fitting Earl jeans and pulled out a crushed packet of Trident.

'Here, have some gum.' She tossed the pack lazily in Jenny's direction.

'Fine.' Jenny popped a piece of spearmint gum in her mouth and straightened the framed poster of van Gogh's *Sunflowers* hanging over her desk. 'But really . . . three minutes. I missed lunch.'

She slid into her desk chair, ignoring the fascinating story behind the acquisition of Callie's newest pair of Costume National boots, and logged into her e-mail. A message from Casey, the hot college freshman from Union she'd met over break at Yvonne Stidder's Upper East Side party, sat open in her in-box. He'd written a flirtatious note Sunday night about not being able to sleep from thinking about her. She smiled to herself. It felt good to be wanted by a college guy. She imagined him lying in his dorm's common room, breathlessly telling his friend he'd fallen head over heels. (Did guys say things like that? Not likely.) After spending the rest of the weekend, post-Casey, eating leftovers from her father's kooky vegan Thanksgiving feast, she was grateful to be back at Waverly Academy.

A new e-mail appeared in Jenny's inbox, from a Waverly e-mail address she didn't recognize. The subject line Popular? intrigued her.

Dear Jenny,

    Hi! Sorry to bother you, as I'm sure you're very busy, but we wanted to ask you a favor. We were talking about our final project for Dr Jackson's freshman film class and Claire was like, 'We should totally make a documentary of a popular Waverly girl.' Basically, we'd like to follow you around and film all the cool things you do in a normal day with your friends. Sort of like a week in the life of a popular girl?

We'd love to start getting footage right away, so please think about it. (And please say yes, please, please, please.)

– Kaitlin Becker, Claire Goodrich, and Izzy Vanderbeek

'You're not going to believe this,' Jenny squealed, leaning back in her chair. She stared at her computer screen. Someone wanted to make a movie about *her*? They thought *she* was the most popular girl in school? Not Tinsley or Brett or Callie or any one of the dozens of taller, thinner, more glamorous girls at Waverly?

'What?' Tinsley swung her legs off the bed and pulled her straight, glossy hair into a bun. Her smooth cheeks had spots of pink on them, and there was a cheerful gleam in her eyes. The glow had been there ever since Yvonne Stidder's Thanksgiving party – ever since Tinsley had made up with Julian McCafferty, the tall, totally adorable freshman. Jenny had never thought that Tinsley was *un*happy until she saw what she looked like *happy*. 'Did Zac Efron finally "friend" you?'

Jenny stuck her tongue out. 'Nooo,' she said, standing up and nonchalantly smoothing out her dark red ABS cords. She grabbed her fuzzy pink and white striped scarf from the hook on the back of the door and casually draped it around her neck. 'I have a fan club.'

'And that's news?' Callie asked dryly, tugging at the waist of her loose-fitting skirt. While Tinsley had been glowing since their return to Waverly, Callie had been cranky. Jenny knew that her breakup with Easy had bummed her out, but she was hoping she'd snap out of it soon enough. 'Everyone at Waverly adores you,' she added, kicking her empty suitcase into the bottom of her closet.

'Please.' Jenny's cheeks flushed, thinking of her not-too-distant encounter with Drew Gately, the senior guy who'd tried to manipulate her into sleeping with him. He didn't exactly adore her – he just liked the idea of deflowering a naïve sophomore. 'You know that's not true.' Then she remembered that she'd actually won the Halloween costume competition – people had voted for *her*. A burst of confidence surged through her as she shook out her loose brown curls and slipped her arms into her short red peacoat, hoping Callie and Tinsley would take the hint. 'A few girls want to make a movie about me for their freshman film class.'

Tinsley flicked off Callie's Bose iPod player and grabbed her dove gray Michael Kors coat, still wet from the snow, from where she'd dropped it on Jenny's bed. 'I thought you'd given up your porn career.'

Callie snickered, finally grabbing her pale beige wool coat from the back of her chair and throwing it on. 'Yeah, I thought Hardbody Humphrey was retired.'

'Ha-ha,' Jenny scoffed back, but the hair on the back of

her neck stood up. Why couldn't Tinsley and Callie ever take her seriously? As much as she liked them, she couldn't help wondering if they were always going to see her as some kind of less-cool imitation of them, a sweet but too-short tagalong they couldn't quite shake. 'It's for a documentary, silly. They want to call it *Popular*, or something like that.'

Tinsley and Callie burst into giggles as the three girls shuffled out the door. 'Seriously?' Callie asked, towering over Jenny in her high-heeled Badgley Mischka ankle boots. 'You're going to let some freshmen follow you around with a video camera?'

'Are they going to follow you to class?' Tinsley piped up, pulling down a red cashmere cap and patting her pockets for her wallet. 'To the gym?'

'To the shower?' Callie snorted, the heels clicking on the damp marble stairway.

'*Popular*,' Tinsley intoned in a movie-phone voice as she pulled on her red leather gloves. 'Starring Jennifer "Hardbody" Humphrey.' She started humming some kind of sleazy, porno-sounding music before she and Callie completely dissolved into laughter.

Jenny sighed heavily and buttoned her coat over her ample chest. They could laugh all they wanted, but just wait until they saw her starring in some arty student film.

Outside, the sharp night air made her shiver. In the distance, she could see the glinting lights of the dining hall, and just the thought of the cheesy lasagna on the menu made her mouth water.

Tinsley lit a cigarette. While smoking was forbidden on Waverly grounds, Tinsley had spent enough cold winters in New England to know that from a distance, the smoke looked like warm breath from warm bodies. 'So, Ms. Vernon, what's it like being a single woman again?'

Callie's face tightened almost imperceptibly at the reference to her recent breakup. She pulled her powder blue earmuffs from her coat pocket and slipped them onto her ears. 'It's awesome,' she replied after a moment, her voice devoid of enthusiasm. 'I love not having to shave my legs. And I can eat whatever I want.'

This time, it was Tinsley and Jenny who exchanged glances. Callie was in no danger of gaining a clothing size anytime soon.

'It was about time.' Tinsley let out a huge breath of smoke. 'You guys were getting totally boring.'

Callie knew Tinsley was just trying to make her feel better, but it annoyed her anyway. 'Of course, as soon as I'm single, you're not,' Callie sniffed, feeling suddenly miserable. Tinsley had her little freshman boy toy Julian now. And Jenny had – well, whomever she wanted. No matter how much Callie tried to convince herself it was fun to be on her own, in truth she totally missed Easy. She'd loved him so much, but staying together while he was at military school had just been so *hard*. She couldn't stand not knowing when – or if – they could be together again. And the promise ring he'd sent her, while incredibly romantic, had been too much. But even though she knew she'd made the right decision, she missed the feeling of knowing someone was thinking about her, or about kissing her. . . .

A coy smile played on Tinsley's lips. 'Chill out, Cal. It's not like I'm getting *married*.'

Callie rolled her eyes. In New York over the break, after being sent the promise ring by Easy, she'd practically picked out her wedding dress from the Vera Wang window, much to Tinsley's amusement. 'That's probably a good thing, since Julian is, like, twelve.'

'Maybe it'll be good for you to be on your own for a while,' Jenny spoke up, her tiny voice cheerful but cautious.

'I know, I know.' Callie shook her head dismissively and rubbed her cold, gloved hands together. 'It's just . . . I'm used to having a boyfriend,' she confessed, realizing it even as she said it. 'Before Easy, there was Brandon.'

'Actually, they kind of overlapped,' Tinsley quipped, flicking her half-finished cigarette into a snowbank. She'd never let Callie forget how she'd hooked up with Easy when she was still dating Brandon. 'And when you were a freshman, you and Ethan Lasser were totally inseparable.'

Even the memory of Ethan Lasser – who was always slipping funny little notes into her mailbox – made a lump form in Callie's throat. She thought of all the fancy dinners Brandon had taken her to at Le Petit Coq on Saturday nights when no parties were going on. And how she and Easy always used to sit in the back row of campus plays and concerts so they could skip out early to make out. Then she thought of having fancy dinners – alone. Going to see horrible student plays or the free Saturday afternoon movies in Berkman-Meier hall – alone. Callie suddenly couldn't recall a single Waverly social event she'd ever attended on her own, and panic seized her. 'I have no idea what it's like to be single at this school,' she said, a heavy sense of dread settling into the pit of her stomach.

Tinsley laughed and rubbed her gloves up and down her arms. Her carefree giggle cut through Callie. *What* was so funny? 'You need to get on some medication,' Tinsley said, tossing snow into the air. 'You act like you don't know how to have a good time. There are more things in life than . . .' Before she could finish, her phone buzzed in her pocket, and she quickly scrambled to pull out her black Nokia.

Callie glanced up at the steps of the dining hall, dreading going inside and having to face everyone. Why did breaking up with Easy make her feel lonely instead of free? She couldn't help but feel sad. The Callie-Easy era was over.

'It's Julian.' Tinsley was unable to keep the giddy grin off her face. 'You girls go in – I'll just be a second.'

'Later,' Callie said coldly, following Jenny up the steps. As they pushed through the heavy oak double doors of the dining hall, Brandon Buchanan called out Jenny's name. She headed over to a table full of boys, and Callie was left standing alone in the doorway, hesitating. The smell of overcooked pasta hit her nose, and suddenly

Callie's unshaven legs felt scratchy in her smooth black tights.

Oh my God, she couldn't help thinking. *I have hairy legs and I'm going to die alone.*

A WAVERLY OWL NEVER GAMBLES . . . UNLESS IT'S A SURE THING.

The whir of the cappuccino machine rose over the hum of study-group chatter in Maxwell Hall. A fire crackled in the massive stone fireplace, and outside the large, arched windows the snow fell steadily down in the dark December evening. Brett Messerschmidt's almond-shaped green eyes scanned the lounge, eyeing the well-dressed Waverly Owls enjoying warm cups of coffee, their snow-covered parkas and peacoats tossed aside temporarily. Now that Thanksgiving break was over, Waverly students were reluctantly starting to prepare for finals.

At last Brett spotted who she'd been looking for. Of course, when she'd sent Sebastian Valenti to grab them a seat, she hadn't meant the overstuffed rust-colored velveteen love seat smack in the middle of the room, directly in the line of vision of every single curious eye at Waverly. But with his shiny black Nikes propped up on the low coffee table, and his black Adidas track jacket unzipped halfway down his chest to reveal a tight white T-shirt, Sebastian looked like he didn't give a shit who saw him.

Brett sighed and walked toward him, stepping carefully over the well-worn Oriental throw rugs, damp with sludge tracked in from outdoors. 'Here.' She handed him one of the two lattes she'd just bought from the coffee bar. 'Congratulations,' she added, a little petulantly.

Sebastian puffed out his chest. 'You know I couldn't have passed that test without you. Have a seat.' He casually slung an arm over the back of the love seat, as if that made it more inviting.

Brett eyed the space on the couch next to him. It seemed . . . well, awfully cozy for a tutor to be sharing a love seat with her tutee, even if she was buying him coffee to celebrate his acing yesterday's Latin exam. But her mind wandered back to Thanksgiving break, when they'd certainly been friendly. Faced with spending the whole holiday with the Coopers, her sister Bree's ridiculously uptight future in-laws from Greenwich, Connecticut, Brett had invited Sebastian over for Thanksgiving dinner to make things more interesting. It had worked – the Coopers had fled quickly, mortified by Sebastian's slicked-back hair and appetite for Mountain Dew. And Brett had actually had a surprising amount of fun hanging out with Sebastian.

Until, that was, he'd overheard Brett telling Bree she'd invited him for the sole purpose of pissing off the Coopers, and he'd stormed out. Which left Brett to show up at his house Sunday morning to apologize and beg for a ride back to Waverly. They'd had a nice time, but it still irked Brett that she'd been forced to say sorry to cocky Sebastian. She had been blatantly in the wrong, of course, but there had been a shift in their balance of power, and now Brett was struggling to level things again.

'Yes, that's true.' Brett sat down primly on the other cushion of the love seat, tugging down the hem of her cap-sleeved heather gray Free People sweaterdress. 'You'd be nothing without your fearless tutor,' she teased, crossing her legs and tapping the toe of her flat black Børn riding boot against the coffee table.

Sebastian leaned back against the cushions and took a long sip from his Waverly logo coffee cup. 'Oh, come on, like you're not getting anything out of this too?' He cocked his head, a satisfied grin on his handsome face. He was a good-looking guy, in spite of his overly greased *Sopranos*-reject hairdo. 'Admit it: you're going to miss me.'

Brett narrowed her eyes at him. 'What are you talking about?'

'Well, I didn't know how to break it to you, but this is gonna be our last study session for a while.'

'Oh, really?' Brett blew across the top of her cup, trying not to sound surprised — and a little rejected. She was the one who had to do all the work here. Getting Sebastian to

memorize flash cards was harder than making your way
through the crowds at Macy's on the day after Thanksgiving.
'You get an A-minus on one test and suddenly you don't
need me anymore?'

'God, it's hot when you get all defensive.' Sebastian
reached out and patted Brett's arm, but she pulled it away
as if she'd been burned.

'Can you stop being a pig for once and just tell me what
you're talking about?'

Sebastian trained his dark brown eyes on her, and she
felt herself squirm. 'I was in Horniman's office this morning,
bragging about my A . . .'

'A-minus,' Brett corrected, leaning back into the corner
of the couch. Mrs Horniman was their shared faculty adviser,
and the one who had roped Brett into tutoring the failing
Sebastian in the first place.

Sebastian rolled his eyes to the vaulted ceiling. 'Right.
Anyway, I was telling Horniman how I hadn't started any
college applications yet, and she—'

'You haven't started your applications yet?' Brett interrupted, astonished. Most seniors had been working on their
apps for *months*. Brett even knew a couple of nerds in the junior
class who had already started drafts of their essays – and not
that she'd admit it to anyone, but she had a whole file in her
computer of brainstormed ideas for her Brown personal essay.
(Everything from 'Why I Went to Boarding School' to 'Life
with Bright Red Hair.' Good thing she still had a year to work
on it.) 'Are you crazy? Deadlines are, like, in a few weeks.'

'God, you even *sound* like her.' Sebastian casually raised a hand and patted down his greased-back hair, which was in no danger of moving. 'She told me it was unacceptable for a Waverly Owl not to apply to college, and said she wanted me to spend the next two weeks "hunkering down" and filling out paperwork.'

'That's probably a good idea.' Brett pressed her lips together, wondering why she felt so out of sorts at the idea of not having to tutor Sebastian anymore. It wasn't as if tutoring was any fun. And she'd have a little more time to concentrate on studying for her own finals. But suddenly, the image of Sebastian, sitting on the floor of her family room, rubbing the ears of her mother's squealing Teacup Chihuahuas, flashed through her mind. She quickly squashed it. 'So where are you applying?'

Sebastian shrugged. 'The Waverly standards. You know. Yale, Cornell, Middlebury.' He glanced at Brett, as if daring her to contradict him. 'Brown. I might as well try, right?'

Brown? Brett pursed her lips. 'If you spend half the time on your applications that you do sculpting your hair, you won't have to even worry about getting in.'

Sebastian chose to ignore her remark. 'I'll be up to my elbows in college guidebooks and applications,' he said, rubbing his chin. He'd been kind of quiet all day, and Brett suddenly realized that maybe he was feeling down about having to fill out college applications? Or maybe . . . over not getting to see her?

'Well,' Brett said slowly, 'if you need help . . .'

'You offering your services, tutor?' A familiar self-satisfied grin covered Sebastian's face, and Brett felt irritated that she actually cared about his future prospects. 'Just be sure to call ahead, so I can get you on the schedule. Nothing fires the ladies up like looking through college apps, eh?'

Brett's back stiffened. How dare he think that she — junior class prefect, straight-A student, one of the hottest girls at Waverly — would *wait in line* to spend time with him? He was such an arrogant prick — or he would be, if the idea of Waverly girls actually lining up outside his door weren't so comically absurd. 'Yeah, right. I'm sure all the girls at Waverly are dying to sit in your room and watch you fill out application forms,' she chided, draining the last of her latte. 'That'll be the day.'

Sebastian leaned forward on the couch. 'You don't think I know what the ladies want?' He studied her face again and Brett had to glance away, staring instead at the massive fireplace. 'Throw a polo shirt on me and all the girls in this place will be clawing each other to get at me. It'll be like the Beatles, circa 1974.'

'The Beatles broke up in 1970, genius,' Brett countered snidely. She examined his too-tight T-shirt, too-tight track jacket, too-greasy hair. All of it screamed *tacky*, and the girls at Waverly tended to prefer guys who subtly smelled like a Ralph Lauren store to those who bathed in Drakkar Noir.

So why was she so worried?

Sebastian waved a hand in her face. 'Whatever. It'll be like the Jonas brothers, circa now.'

Brett burst out laughing. Somehow Sebastian always knew how to derail her line of argument. '*Whatever* is right.' Brett smirked. 'I'll believe it when I see it.'

'So beautiful, so skeptical.' Sebastian shook his head mockingly. 'I just love to prove you wrong, Red.'

'I won't hold my breath.' Brett glanced up to see Benny Cunningham staring at her and Sebastian. She couldn't imagine someone like Benny, with her pearl drop earrings, her two-hundred-million-dollar trust fund, and her blue-blooded Philadelphia heritage, ever giving Sebastian the time of day. Maybe it would be good for his ego – his massive ego – for him to be proven so devastatingly wrong.

'A friendly wager,' he insisted, holding out his hand.

Brett glanced down. A shiny gold watch hung loosely on his wrist. This was going to be even easier than she'd thought.

A WAVERLY OWL DOES NOT ENGAGE IN PUBLIC FORNICATION.

Tinsley blinked as her eyes adjusted to the darkness of the Rhinecliff Lucky Strike later that night. The fluorescent lighting flooded the bowling lanes and carpeted lobby with a urine-colored light. The lanes were half-filled with blue-haired ladies in matching shirts, a couple of families with crying kids, and groups of beer-bellied men in too-small tees. Tinsley groaned audibly. The bowling alley was a place where many Waverly Owls ended up on Friday nights when there was nothing better to do, but in Tinsley's opinion, there was *always* something better to do. She'd been dragged here a dozen times in her three years at Waverly, but never had she come willingly. Until, that is, Julian McCafferty invited her. It was sad but true: she couldn't deny the boy anything.

She slipped out of her long gray coat and hung it on a rickety, almost empty coatrack in the corner. The heels of her Miss Sixty oxford pumps sank into the thick carpeting as if it were quicksand. The whole *place* seemed to be covered in carpeting – the walls, even the ceiling – that reeked of smoke. Against the far wall, she spotted the dimly lit bar, the bar stools filled with overweight townies in butt crack–revealing jeans downing beers. Tinsley was wondering what on earth she was doing in this smelly, tacky place when a familiar head popped up from behind a rack of bowling balls. Julian's shaggy blond-brown hair was still damp from a shower and curled slightly around his ears. He caught her eye and smiled, and the tiny dimple at the corner of his lips appeared. Tinsley's knees trembled.

'I always feel like I've gone back in time when I come in here.' Tinsley waltzed down the two steps into the little seating alcove where Julian stood. In his dark gray boot-cut corduroys, faded black White Stripes T-shirt, and green cardigan sweater, he looked hopelessly adorable.

'Yeah, it's kind of old school.' Julian leaned forward, his warm brown eyes taking in Tinsley's whole face, and planted a soft kiss on her cheek. She closed her eyes, enjoying the smell of his woodsy-scented shower gel. It made her want to get even closer to him. 'But it's perfect now.'

'It is,' Tinsley replied huskily, stepping closer to Julian and planting her lips fully on his mouth. As they kissed, the whole rest of the world disappeared – the fat guys at the bar, the nasty carpeted walls, the poor boyfriendless people back at Waverly.

Tinsley had never expected to be grateful to dorky senior Yvonne Stidder for anything in her life. But it was only after spending Thanksgiving snowbound at Yvonne's town house in New York with a group of other Owls, Julian included, that she'd been able to secure her second chance with him. The Friday after Thanksgiving, she and Julian both decided to head back to Waverly early, having nowhere else to go. Being practically alone with Julian on campus was delicious. They trudged through the unplowed snow to the diner in town, and sledded down Goat's Hill on garbage can lids stolen from Dining Services. They spent the evenings in the Cinephiles film room in the basement of Hopkins Hall, drinking hot chocolate and Baileys and watching old movies. It had been about midway through *To Catch a Thief*, when Cary Grant and Grace Kelly were bantering sexily on the screen, that Julian had leaned over and kissed Tinsley. Weeks and weeks had gone by since they'd last hooked up, but Tinsley hadn't forgotten the warm, honey taste of his lips.

'Mmm,' Julian pulled away slowly, bringing Tinsley back to earth. 'You need shoes.' He already had his red-and-brown clownlike bowling shoes laced up, his black Vans tucked neatly under the plastic bench.

The idea of wearing such ridiculous shoes made Tinsley's skin crawl. They looked like something a blind, crack-addicted designer on *Project Runway* might call 'authentic'. 'Do you have any idea how many feet have been in those?'

Julian shrugged, his amused eyes focused on Tinsley's lips. She wondered if he was thinking about kissing her again. 'You wear secondhand clothes, don't you? It's the same thing.'

Tinsley's lips twitched under the scrutiny. 'Correction: I wear vintage. And wearing a vintage Chanel dress is not the same as wearing a pair of bowling shoes that league ladies sweat in once a week.' She stuck her tongue out at Julian but grabbed a pair of sevens from the gray-haired woman at the shoe counter. Once her yellow-and-red-patched shoes were on her feet, she modeled them for Julian, holding out a leg and pretending they looked sexy with her black Earl jeans. 'Should we just get it over with and join a league?'

'I think you have to be good to join a league,' Julian answered, grinning as he plopped a pink bowling ball in Tinsley's hands.

'You're good,' she protested, dropping her favorite art nouveau wire ring into the pocket of her jeans for safe-keeping.

Julian tucked Tinsley's hair behind her left ear, and her heart beat faster, hoping he was going in for another kiss. 'It's not me I'm worried about.' A couple in their thirties with two whining children stared at them from a couple of lanes down – probably pining for the days when they were young and hot and not saddled with two snot-nosed brats.

'That's it,' Tinsley mock-scowled, tossing her hair and

stepping onto the polished hardwood of the lane. 'I'm throwing spares today.'

'You mean strikes.' Julian picked up a swirly green bowling ball. 'Watch this.' He tiptoed toward the lane and then in one long graceful motion extended his arm, releasing the ball so that it skittered across the worn wooden lanes. The pins all fell as if by magic.

'You didn't tell me you grew up in a bowling alley,' Tinsley complained lightly, smiling.

'My next-door neighbor in Seattle had a lane in his base-ment,' Julian confessed, walking back and casually tracing a finger against Tinsley's knee, almost making her pass out. She'd read somewhere – *Cosmo*, maybe? – that the knees were one of the great, underappreciated erogenous zones. She'd always been skeptical about *Cosmo*'s 'research depart-ment', but suddenly she was a believer. 'We'd spend all our time down there, bowling and watching the *Lord of the Rings* movies.'

'Just the two of you?' Tinsley teased. She didn't know too much about Julian's life in Seattle, before Waverly, and she wanted to know it all. She'd only been to Seattle once, and it rained the whole time.

'We were kind of dorks.' Julian yawned, and Tinsley could see a filling in his back molar. 'If you can imagine that.'

Tinsley smiled as she stood and made her way toward the lane, swishing her hips as she walked for Julian's viewing pleasure. She liked the idea of Julian spending his free time with his dorky neighbor, bowling the afternoons away instead of chasing girls the way someone like Heath Ferro had probably done since puberty. Julian wasn't consumed with sex the way Heath was, and that made him seem so much more grown up, despite his age, than the rest of the Waverly boys.

Most of all, she loved the way Julian looked at her, not like he was wondering what she looked like naked, but wondering what she was thinking, or what she might say.

But it still made her want to get naked with him.

Fifteen minutes later, Tinsley had knocked over only a handful of pins – not that she cared – while Julian had bowled like a professional. He held up his hand to get a high five after throwing another strike. Tinsley laced her fingers through his and pulled him down to the hard plastic bench. She kissed him on the cheek, her lips resting there a moment longer than necessary.

'Get a room,' a ten-year-old kid called as he ran by to the bathroom. *Not a bad idea*, Tinsley thought.

'Well,' Julian said softly, 'I'm going to try for strikes every time if that's the reward.' He ran his fingers on the inside of her forearm and she felt the electricity surge through her body. She'd never been this into anyone for as long as she could remember. Not even Chiedo, the sexy college student she'd hooked up with in South Africa, whose face was becoming fuzzier and fuzzier as the weeks slipped by. Tinsley just stared at him, distracted by the slow realization that Julian might be the guy she'd lose her virginity to.

She instantly imagined their two bodies intertwined on a set of sheets, dusk falling outside the window. The fact that Julian was a freshman and that they'd be losing it to each other gave the image an extra sweetness that Tinsley hadn't previously considered. She'd had plenty of chances to lose it before, but now she thanked the virginity gods that she'd waited.

'Another game?' he asked, straightening up and leaning against the back of the bench. She hadn't realized they'd played a whole one. 'Or do you want to get something to eat?'

Tinsley had forgotten about food entirely, her body craving only one thing. She glanced around her toward the other lanes, which had suddenly grown silent. The kids from a couple lanes over had disappeared, and the parents were making out like wild animals on the plastic bench. 'I hope they're not going to do it right here,' Tinsley laughed, pointing them out to Julian.

'Where's the "get a room" kid when you need him?' Julian laughed, too, as he put their bowling balls back on the rack. 'He should definitely check them into a hotel.'

'Is that how you'd do it?' Tinsley asked innocently, kicking off her gross bowling shoes and brushing his leg with her foot.

'Well, there are easier ways.' He shrugged, unlacing his own shoes and sliding his feet into his Vans. He tickled the bottom of Tinsley's foot lightly.

'Yeah? How would you know?' She'd meant the question

as a flirty tease, just another in a long afternoon of flirty teases. But it came out with a hint of jealous suspicion she hadn't expected.

'I've got a little experience in that area,' he confessed, touching his hemp necklace.

Tinsley pulled her foot away from Julian's tickling fingers and leaned over to grab her own shoes, letting her dark, smooth hair fall in front of her face, hiding it from his view. 'Experience doing what?' She kept her voice cool, but she felt anything but. Was Julian trying to say he'd *slept* with someone before? He was fifteen – that wasn't even *legal* in most civilized states.

Tinsley looked up and into Julian's wide brown eyes, which suddenly weren't as innocent as she'd previously thought. A shy smile played on his lips, but for once, Tinsley was unmoved by his dimple. 'Experience doing exactly what I'd like to do with you someday.'

Tinsley flicked her long hair over her shoulder. Instead of exciting her, Julian's words sent a chill down her spine.

'You'll have better luck sticking with bowling,' she said calmly, getting to her feet and flouncing to the front counter, bowling shoes in hand. But her flesh was on fire. When the *hell* had Julian lost his virginity?

And, more important, whom had he lost it *to*?

 **OwlNet**

From: GeraldWilde@waverly.edu
TO: BrettMesserschmidt@waverly.edu
Date: Wednesday, December 4, 7:28 A.M.
Subject: Important assignment

Dear Brett,

Hope you had a great Thanksgiving break and are ready to finish off the semester!

Would you mind stopping by my office this morning or afternoon? As our junior class prefect, I've got a special project for you to spearhead. Don't worry, it's not a typical assignment, and I have a feeling you'll find it very rewarding.

Best,

G. W.

4

**A WAVERLY OWL KNOWS THAT THE TRUTH IS
SOMETIMES HARDER TO BELIEVE THAN A LIE.**

Brandon Buchanan strode across the Waverly Academy dining hall on Wednesday afternoon with a tray full of food, feeling more confident than he had in weeks – months, even. All he could think about since he'd hooked up with Helga Dunderdorf over Thanksgiving break, was, well, Helga Dunderdorf. Or, rather, Hellie Dunderdorf. That first night, when Brandon was tracing his finger across her flat, milky-white stomach, Hellie murmured, 'Call me Hellie. All my friends do. Helga makes me sound like a Viking.'

Hellie was one of Professor Dunderdorf's gorgeous and brilliant twin daughters. She and her sister went to the exclusive Le Rosey boarding school in Switzerland but had been home for the break. Heath Ferro, Brandon's shamelessly

horny roommate, had managed to procure an invite to
Professor Dunderdorf's Thanksgiving dinner, having heard
of the sisters' legendary hotness. Brandon and Hellie had
hit it off immediately, and they'd wound up kissing in her
bed on Thanksgiving night. Then on Friday night, Brandon
managed to climb a ladder into Hellie's attic room – barely
dirtying his Brooks Brothers chinos in the process – for
another intense night together. It was insane. The whole
weekend had passed by in a blur of very un-Brandon-
Buchanan-like activity. Only now, three days after kissing
Hellie goodbye, was he starting to come down from his
cloud. But he was coming down as a changed man.

The dining hall buzzed with lunchtime activity, and
Brandon spotted Lon Baruzza, Alan St Girard, Ryan
Reynolds, and Heath crowded around the round table smack
in the center of the room. They claimed it offered the best
girl-watching positions, and indeed, as Brandon strode up
to the table, the boys' eyes were glued to Trisha Reikken's
obscenely short plaid miniskirt as she leaned over the salad
bar. Brandon set his tray down next to Lon. 'Shove over,
will you?'

Lon glanced up at Brandon in surprise before shifting
over to make room. The dark-haired senior scholarship kid
had an oversize nose, which somehow served, for the Waverly
girls, as evidence of his other oversized body parts. Brandon
suspected that Lon had started the rumor himself.

'Lamest Thanksgiving ever,' Teague Williams interrupted
as he gracelessly dropped his tray onto the table, sending

splashes of orange Gatorade across everyone's plates. Teague was a tall redheaded senior on the swim team who always smelled like he just got out of the pool. 'My sister was going to set me up with her roommate at Smith, but she turned out to be a total dog. I spent most of the weekend hiding in my room with my Wii.'

'Dude.' Heath soaked a piece of French bread in his plateful of overcooked spaghetti and popped the whole thing in his mouth. 'You know those Smith chicks are all pent-up nymphos. You should have hit that!'

'Right?' Ryan ran his hand across the sorry-looking thatch of stubble that had appeared on his chin over break. Combined with his ill-conceived platinum eyebrow stud, the stubble made him look like some kind of low-budget pimp. 'Just keep the lights off.'

Everyone laughed. Brandon normally would have added some scathing criticism to their blatantly moronic chatter, but he was in too good a mood. He bit into his tomato and mozzarella sandwich, careful to avoid leaking pesto onto his pressed Burberry flat-front trousers. Hellie had gone back to Switzerland on Sunday, but she'd been texting him pictures of her school world – the medieval château at the center of campus where she took her Latin classes, her sunny, slope-ceilinged dorm room with a poster of a Botticelli painting on the wall, the dance studio where she took ballet three times a week. She'd even taken a picture of herself, looking unbearably sexy, in the faded gray T-shirt with a Le Rosey crest and the boxer shorts she wore to sleep. Which only made Brandon wish even more that she were sleeping next to him.

'Dude, I would have come back to Waverly before I let some ugly Smith chick push me around,' Lon declared.

'Yeah, like I was going to spend Thanksgiving on campus,' Teague snorted, flicking a crumb off his black button-down. It would have looked good if it had ever seen an iron. 'And what? Play spin the bottle with the international students? Eat me.'

'You guys don't know what you missed,' Brandon offered between bites, waiting for the others to ask him about Hellie. Although he normally wasn't a bragger, he was kind of excited to have, for once, something to brag about.

'You bring back any Thanksgiving leftovers?' Ryan asked Alan. He pinched his thumb and forefinger together and brought them to his lips, inhaling. Alan's parents were infamous around campus for running their own marijuana farm in the backwoods of New Hampshire – for medicinal purposes, of course.

Alan stroked the brown scruff under his chin and smiled dolefully. 'Enough to keep me stuffed for a month. Maybe more.'

'Righteous.' Ryan nodded. He pushed his dirty lunch tray to the center of the table. He had an annoying habit of 'forgetting' to take his tray to the tray return, instead leaving it on the table for the overworked dining services staff to take care of.

'Heath and I stayed back, didn't he tell you?' Brandon

asked the table in a moment of silence while everyone stuffed their faces with food.

Lon and Ryan exchanged glances. 'Yeah, heard about the, uh . . . Swedish model.' Lon leaned back in his chair and popped a couple of grapes into his mouth.

'She's Swiss, actually,' Brandon corrected Lon. He munched on a couple of chips while the rest of the table waited for him to regale them with Tales of the Sauna. He anticipated their congratulations as eagerly as he did Hellie's next pic. 'And she's not a model . . . although she could be.'

'*Swiss* model, right,' Ryan said, thumping the heel of his hand into his forehead. 'We stand corrected.' Alan St Girard chuckled, then crammed a forkful of mashed potatoes into his mouth to hide it.

Teague covered his mouth and coughed, 'Bullshit.'

Brandon set down his fork. What the fuck? 'Dude, trust me. She was totally hot.' He glanced up for backup from Heath, but he'd disappeared to refill his Sprite glass.

'If by "hooking up with a Swedish model" you mean you "beat it to pics from Victoria's Secret all weekend," then . . .' Ryan trailed off, smirking.

'Dude, she's *Swiss*,' Teague corrected him, shoveling a forkful of salad into his mouth.

'Oh, right. My mistake.' Ryan leered at Brandon and the others chuckled at the joke.

'You don't believe me?' Brandon asked, suddenly getting that these guys weren't teasing him because they were jealous – but because they thought he was making it all up. His face flushed and he tugged at the collar of his Ben Sherman shirt. 'Ask Heath.'

'You're asking us to believe a guy who claims he sat next to Miley Cyrus on a flight to LA and she let him feel her up in the bathroom?' Ryan snorted loudly, and Brandon thought about how satisfying it would be to give him a black eye. 'Just please tell me that you didn't share the same catalog.'

Lon coughed up the last of his Diet Coke and Alan slapped him on the back a couple of times. 'Take it easy, baby.'

Brandon considered whipping out his cell to show him the scrapbook of flesh-baring photos quickly filling up the memory in his Nokia, but he didn't want to give them the satisfaction. After all, why should these douchebags get to partake in Hellie's heavenly beauty simply for doubting and mocking him? No way.

'If you're going to Switzerland over Christmas, will you get me one of the cuckoo clocks with the little dude who comes out and hits something with a hammer?' Teague asked, his lazy green eyes amused. 'I think that would look good in my room.'

Brandon grabbed his tray, his knuckles white with rage. The conversation had devolved into an argument about whether or not Miley Cyrus was actually a virgin. None of them noticed as Brandon slunk away, his forehead burning with frustration. As he returned the tray to the kitchen, he caught sight of Heath sitting at a table with Brett

Messerschmidt and Sage Francis, his arms waving in the air and his mouth wide open. For a second, Brandon thought he must be talking up Brandon's artful seduction of the Swiss sexpot in front of Sage, Brandon's ex-girlfriend. It was about time Heath did something for him.

But then he saw that Heath was just trying to look down Brett's shirt, and he realized he was going to have to fight his own battles.

A WAVERLY OWL KNOWS THAT THERE ARE PLENTY OF FISH IN THE SEA — YOU JUST HAVE TO KEEP THROWING BACK THE LOSERS.

On Wednesday afternoon, Callie Vernon dropped her pale blue pleated Tocca peacoat onto one of the coat pegs that lined the foyer of the dining hall. She took a deep breath and strode into the crowded lunchroom, scanning the crowd for familiar faces. Even though Easy Walsh hadn't been at Waverly since he had been expelled more than a month ago, she couldn't help looking for his face whenever she walked into a room. It was a reflex.

When she'd been dating Easy, it had seemed like there were practically hundreds of hot, available Waverly boys eyeing her from the fringes, waiting until she was single again. Now it was time to pick one. In her new gray wool Alice + Olivia minidress and fringed suede Roberto Cavalli boots, she knew that finding a new boy shouldn't be too hard.

She spotted Brett, sitting at a crowded table by one of the enormous stained glass windows next to Benny Cunningham and Sage Francis. Benny's green cowl-neck sweater made her look like a leprechaun, and Sage, since she'd dumped Brandon Buchanan, had reverted back to wearing far too much makeup. Neither of them was much competition. Callie grabbed a tray, still warm from the dishwasher, and tossed her wavy strawberry blond hair over her shoulder as she halfheartedly passed through the food line.

A tall, borderline-cute sophomore boy narrowly avoided running into her with a tray piled high with grilled cheese sandwiches and french fries. 'Watch where you're going, *chica*,' the sophomore muttered rudely under his breath. Callie blinked. Since when were unattractive underlings rude to *her*? Maybe she'd underestimated the difficulty of finding a datable Waverly boy.

She threw some mesclun greens onto her plate and sprinkled some chunks of feta on top. But as she plopped a couple of plump cherry tomatoes onto her salad, a strange image flashed before her eyes: Easy Walsh, maybe fifteen years from now, still with his stunningly crooked smile but with laugh lines and broader shoulders, living happily on a Kentucky horse farm. The vision was complete with racehorses and a down-to-earth Kentucky girl with long, light-brown hair and hands that weren't afraid of getting dirty. She saw him

popping fresh garden tomatoes into the girl's mouth – skank!
– and the two of them rocking together on the front porch
while the sun set behind a giant maple tree.

'Is something wrong with the tomatoes?' Emmy
Rosenblum asked, wrinkling her nose and looking at the
tiny cherry tomatoes Callie had unconsciously picked from
her salad and left sitting on the edge of the salad bar.

'I, uh, thought I saw a bug on one,' Callie muttered,
grabbing her tray and heading for the soda machine. She
filled a plastic cup with ice water and tried to calm her
beating heart.

Why was she acting like such a freak? How hard could
it be to find a guy, really? Waverly was fifty-two percent
male, according to the statistics on the Web site, so the
odds were in her favor. Callie filled another glass with Diet
Coke and surveyed the room for the best-looking guys.
Immediately, her eyes lit on Brandon Buchanan carrying his
tray to the tray return. Yes, Brandon was gorgeous, in an
overly put-together, ironed-his-underwear kind of way, but
he was *Brandon*. She'd been down that road and just couldn't
be with someone who used more beauty products than she
did. She needed someone who was as good-looking as
Brandon but with an edge.

Her eyes rested on Alan St Girard, sitting at the table
Brandon had just vacated. She briefly considered him: he
was kind of cute, and he hung out with the right people.
He'd dated Alison Quentin, the pretty Korean girl on her
floor in Dumbarton, for a few months, so he had decent

taste in girls. The scruff would have to go immediately, of course, but all that would take was a razor. She fantasized that underneath the layers of long-sleeve thermal shirts and the fog of stale pot smoke, he was a gold mine.

Except, Callie remembered miserably, he'd been Easy's roommate. Which meant whenever she sneaked into his room, she'd be faced with Easy's empty bed and would think of Easy, and the look on his face atop the Empire State Building.

As Callie fumbled to pick a fork and knife from the silverware tubs, her hazel eyes narrowed in on Parker Dubois. He sat alone at a small table with a book open in front of him. He was the impossibly hot senior that everyone pretended was from Belgium, though she knew he was really American with a French dad. There was even a rumor that he was descended from European royalty. She watched as Parker ran his fingers through his golden brown hair and turned a page in his book. Suddenly Callie realized she'd never, not once, seen him flirting with a girl. He *had* to be gay.

Heath Ferro, who'd planted himself next to Brett, stood up and called, 'Princess! Over here!' Callie fought a surge of irritation – like she needed him to wave her over to Brett's table. At that exact moment, a beam of sunlight shot through the stained glass window and struck Heath's jawline. He looked handsome, standing there in a navy blue crew-neck sweater fitted around his toned soccer body.

But ew. Did she really want to end up on YouTube in

some homemade porno made with a handheld device hidden in Heath's closet? Heath would do for an emergency make-out session if she got really desperate, but he was *far* from boyfriend material.

Callie dropped her tray onto the heavy oak table and slid into the empty chair next to Brett. 'Hey,' she greeted everyone glumly.

Benny nudged Callie's tray with a long, unpolished fingernail. Callie's plate of lime Jell-O cubes jiggled. 'How can you eat that stuff, Cal? It's made of gelatin, which is, you know, made from the jelly in pigs' hooves.'

Heath reached over and stabbed one of Callie's Jell-O cubes with his fork. He popped it in his mouth defiantly. 'Mmm, pig hooves.'

Callie focused her eyes on her salad, but her mind wandered. Maybe she'd have to date a teacher . . . or a townie, she thought despairingly. Her parents had been high school sweethearts, and her mother was always reminding her that Waverly was the perfect place to find a husband. *Soul mate*, she nauseatingly called it. For the longest time, she'd been convinced that Easy was the one . . . but she'd clearly been wrong about that. The whole thing made tears of frustration spring to her eyes, but she pressed her eyelids together to keep them from smudging her olive green Benefit eyeliner.

When her eyes opened again, they focused on the door to the dining hall – and the gorgeous guy with floppy black hair and chiseled features coming through it at that exact moment, as if by fate. Her eyes scanned the well-built athletic body, hidden under a pair of dark, pressed khakis and a navy blue Ralph Lauren polo shirt.

Who. Was. *That?*

'Who *is* that?' Callie whispered under her breath, trying to disguise the urgency of her question by nibbling on a sliced cucumber. She felt faint. This was exactly how it happened in movies. Just when the heroine was at her most desperate, in walked her savior.

The tone in Callie's voice made Brett immediately put down her tuna sandwich. 'Who?' She whirled around to see who Callie was talking about. Standing beside a table of seniors, Sebastian reached out and grabbed a french fry off Celine Colista's plate. In his polo and khakis – which he must have run out and bought immediately after their conversation yesterday – he might have looked like any other athletic Waverly guy. But with his dark, thick hair totally devoid of gel and falling lazily across his forehead, highlighting his dark brown eyes, he looked . . . totally transformed. And amazingly . . . gorgeous.

'Ohmigod!' Benny pressed her elbow into Brett's side, her pink-glossed lips falling open in disbelief. 'That's totally your greaser!'

'That *can't* be Sebastian,' Sage whispered, taking in the scene.

Brett leaned back against the hard slats of her chair and crossed her arms over her chest. Okay, so maybe Sebastian was half right. He certainly had managed to call attention to himself with his new look, but that didn't *mean* anything.

As soon as he started talking, all the Waverly girls would realize he was still the same sexist, maddeningly lazy Sebastian Valenti.

But before she could say a word, Callie, Benny, and Sage had all scooted away from the table. 'I forgot – I wanted to talk to Celine about something,' Callie announced deviously, heading in Sebastian's direction with Sage and Benny on her heels.

Brett found herself rolling her eyes and turning away, not wanting to see the girls fawning over Sebastian – his prophecy fulfilled. She knew, of course, that he was doing it more to annoy her than to actually impress the ladies, though he looked like he was clearly enjoying the newfound attention. When she glanced up, he was talking to Benny Cunningham, but his eyes were on Brett. He tilted his head at her and mouthed a *What's up?* She quickly glanced away, pretending she hadn't seen.

'You know that dude?' Heath asked, peeling back a banana and taking a giant chomp. He stared enviously at Sebastian. 'He's got like six chicks all over him and he just came in the door!'

'I'm late for a meeting.' Brett glanced at her antique silver watch. She had six minutes to get over to Hopkins Hall. While she'd been annoyed before about having to meet Mr Wilde, who'd recently been promoted to DC adviser, she was grateful for the excuse to leave the dining hall. The last thing she wanted to do was watch Sebastian gloat about how right he'd been. She ditched her tray and grabbed her short, gunmetal gray quilted Diesel jacket from the coat pegs. She zipped it up and sauntered out the foyer without a second glance at Sebastian and his merry band of followers.

If he was trying to annoy her, it was a good start.

From: JennyHumphrey@waverly.edu
TO: RufusHumphrey@poetsonline.com
Date: Wednesday, December 4, 12:12 P.M.
Subject: Jenny Humphrey, movie star!

Dear Dad,

Just kidding. Sort of. Some freshmen girls asked if they could make a documentary about *moi* for their film class! How cool is that? It's because they think I live a glamorous life or something – it's all very flattering. I promise not to reveal any embarrassing family secrets – like how my father wears rainbow-colored suspenders – so don't worry. Although actually, you'd probably love that.

And no, I'm not neglecting my schoolwork, I swear. Finals are coming up, and I think I'm pretty ready for them. Oh and I'm sending you some pics of the snow-covered campus. It's pretty amazing. In the city, the snow's always brown – but here it's actually white!

Love you lots. Hugs and hair balls to Marx, too.

Jenny

6

A WAVERLY OWL DOESN'T LOOK A GIFT HORSE IN
THE MOUTH.

The door to Mr Wilde's office on the second floor of Hopkins Hall was half-open, and the sounds of Radiohead obscured Brett's knock. Gerald Wilde was the popular history teacher who'd taken over the Disciplinary Committee after Eric Dalton, the young Latin teacher with whom Brett had unwisely had an affair, had been 'let go' earlier in the semester. Brett poked her head in the doorway and saw Mr Wilde sitting at his desk, his brow furrowed as he scribbled something on a pile of papers. He looked young enough to be a college student – in fact, he'd been the resident hot young teacher on campus before Eric Dalton showed up.

He jumped slightly when Brett knocked a second time, and stood up to wave her in. The office was about half the size of a typical Waverly dorm room – or about twice the size of a broom closet. Ceiling-high bookshelves were stuffed with books and folders with papers spilling out of them. She fought off a dizzying surge of claustrophobia.

'Brett! Thanks so much for coming!' Mr Wilde rubbed his hand against his forehead and looked as if he'd forgotten why he'd asked her to come in the first place.

'Am I late?' Brett asked politely, sliding into the padded chair facing the desk and promptly banging her knee into it. Faced with the DC adviser's poorly chosen purplish button-down shirt, Brett felt slightly too dressy in her hunter green pleated Anna Sui skirt and silky white peasant shirt.

'No, of course not.' Mr Wilde took a giant gulp of water from a green plastic cup on his desk, and Brett realized it was also about a thousand degrees in here. She unconsciously wiped a hand against her forehead. 'You've been nominated for a special role.' Mr Wilde smiled as he pushed his chair back from his desk. He made it sound about as appealing as *You've been nominated to clean the toilets.*

'To do what?' Brett asked cautiously, crossing her legs and taking care not to kick the desk again. The last time she'd been called in for a 'special role', it had been to tutor Sebastian. A slight breeze blew in through the window, cooling Brett's skin.

'Relax,' Mr Wilde said, grinning. 'It's actually kind of fun.' He reached into his top desk drawer and riffled through a mess of papers and CD cases without covers, finally fishing out a stack of spreadsheets. 'You're in charge of organizing this year's Secret Santa exchange.'

Brett had almost forgotten it was Secret Santa time, the allegedly community-building exercise that covered the two weeks leading up to Waverly's annual black tie Holiday Ball. The whole campus got involved, everyone sneaking secret gifts into each other's mailboxes or dorm rooms. 'Isn't that Emily Strauss's job?' Brett asked, suddenly surprised that it was so close to Christmas. Where had the semester gone? 'She's the senior prefect.'

Mr Wilde shook his head. 'Traditionally it *is* the senior prefect's responsibility,' he answered, and Brett could tell from the way he was carefully choosing his words that Emily had bailed. 'But Emily is, uh, especially busy with college applications at this point in the school year, and wanted a little help with some of the senior prefect holiday responsibilities.' Brett was familiar with Emily Strauss's unwavering desire to get into Yale, because she never shut up about it. 'Basically, you'll assign every Waverly Owl a Secret Santa and then supervise the whole process as it unfolds. And you'll help plan the actual party itself. What do you think?'

Brett fidgeted. Between studying for finals, completing her other DC responsibilities, and prepping for the SATs, she was supposed to squeeze in taking charge of the whole Secret Santa process? Hadn't she done the administration enough favors when she took on tutoring Sebastian at Mrs Horniman's insistence? And look how *that* had turned out.

'There are a number of important alums attending the ball,' Mr Wilde reminded her, tapping a pen against the edge of his desk. 'So we really need someone who can come through on this.' He lowered his eyes at Brett.

Brett nodded slowly, understanding that she didn't have a choice. She was getting used to that feeling. But the Holiday Ball was less than two weeks away – Emily must have done some of the planning already, right? 'Sure,' Brett said, suddenly realizing this was a blessing in disguise. She actually kind of welcomed the distraction – a new project was the perfect way to ignore Sebastian's annoying sociological experiment.

'Excellent.' A look of relief washed over Mr Wilde's face as he handed the stack of spreadsheets to Brett. 'Here's a list of the student body for Secret Santa pairing. Go to it, and let me know if you have any questions.'

She took the ream of paper and stuffed it into her worn leather Chloé tote bag, eager to escape the confines of Mr Wilde's office. It wasn't until later that afternoon, when she had the spreadsheets fanned across two tables at CoffeeRoasters in Rhinecliff that she realized what an enormous undertaking it was to pair students up for the Secret Santa exchange. Should she give only freshmen to freshmen? Girls to girls? Wasn't there some way to just have a computer do it randomly? It was the twenty-first century, after all.

The tables shook as Heath Ferro appeared out of nowhere and slid into an armchair across from Brett, his black puffy North Face parka jostling some papers onto the floor.

He eyed the spreadsheets of names, his greenish eyes wide with glee, as he unwrapped a hideous red and yellow striped scarf from his neck. 'So I hear you're Santa Claus!'

Brett scrambled to collect all the papers and flipped them over. 'Shhh,' she hissed, glancing around her. Mr Wilde had told her to keep quiet about the Secret Santa – as if it were a matter of national security. She took a sip of her cappuccino, cold at this point, and gave Heath an icy glare. 'Apparently.'

'Want a little helper?' he asked, oblivious to Brett's annoyance as he tried to peek under one of the papers.

'No!' Brett snatched them all up in her arms, shielding them from Heath's prying. 'There's a reason it's called *Secret Santa*.'

'I could really sex this thing up for you, if you want,' he offered, brushing the snow out of his shaggy dark blond hair. 'I mean, it's totally lame, right? Some dork gives you some present you could only give a cousin you don't really know – a gift certificate for the snack bar, maybe one of those Waverly owl key chains, lottery scratch tickets—'

'You're not allowed to give scratch tickets,' she said automatically, only half-listening, as she stuffed the papers into her bag.

'That's what I'm *talking* about!' Heath squirmed in his chair as if she'd agreed with what he was saying. 'Let's make it all about what you're *not* supposed to do.'

Brett threw her pen down on the table, slightly amused

at Heath's childish enthusiasm for the Secret Santa gift exchange. 'They should've put *you* in charge of this,' she suggested, only half-joking.

'I'm not so good with responsibility. But this ship needs a rudder, and that's you,' Heath declared. 'This is the perfect opportunity to shake up the system.' He rubbed his hands together, and with his cheeks flushed red from the cold, Brett could kind of see why Kara Whalen had gone out with him. 'What if everyone took nude pictures of themselves from the waist down and exchanged them? And everyone had to guess who their Secret *Naked* Santa was?'

Brett shot him a contemptuous look. It was also kind of easy to see why Kara had dumped him. 'I don't think so.'

'Okay, okay.' Heath was nonplussed. 'That idea's not for you. I got a million of them, though.' He closed his eyes, conjuring up his next dirty proposal. 'Oh! This is perfect: what if everyone gave coupons for a free hookup, to be redeemed at a time and place of our choosing? Someplace dark. We could use the old—'

'You're insane, you know that?' Brett asked, getting to her feet. She slung her heavy bag over her shoulder and realized she'd need to hole up at an empty desk on the third floor of the library if she actually wanted to get anything done.

Heath sighed. 'I can see you're going to make this difficult,' he said, scratching his head with his hand as if Brett were the nuisance, not him.

'And I can see you're going to try to distract me from my job,' she shot back. She wound her white pashmina around her neck.

'Easy, tiger.' A wounded look crossed Heath's face, but Brett knew him too well to be fooled. Nothing really bothered him – at least, nothing besides Kara dumping him. Heath seemed to care so little about anything besides having a good time, and yet, he'd been so unexpectedly crushed when Kara told him she didn't want to go out with him anymore last month. Brett remembered seeing him, vodka-soaked and miserable, staring forlornly at pictures of the two of them in happier times. Brett knew what it was like to get dumped – in fact, it was that same night that Jeremiah Mortimer, her on-again-off-again boyfriend, had dumped her for the last time. It made her feel kind of sorry for Heath.

Kind of. 'I've got to get to work.' Brett zipped up her coat and adjusted her messenger bag.

Heath ran a hand over his hair and slunk back in his armchair, smiling his infuriatingly satisfied smile – as if he knew a secret no one else did. 'Don't be such a Grinch.'

'Don't be such a pervert. It's getting really old.' Brett spun on her heel and stalked out of the coffee shop. Outside, snowflakes were slowly falling and melting onto the pavement. Pretty holiday decorations hung from the cast iron lampposts that lined Main Street, and couples carrying over-stuffed shopping bags strolled down the sidewalk, holding hands. A cluster of Girl Scouts were singing 'Jingle Bells' on the steps to the First Presbyterian Church.

Brett took a deep breath of cold fresh air and stuffed her bare hands into the pockets of her coat. What she really wanted this holiday was to win a certain bet.

TO GET THE TRUTH, A WISE OWL GOES TO THE
SOURCE — OR AT LEAST, TO HIS ROOM.

An arctic wind whipped across the common on Wednesday evening, but Tinsley barely felt the cold against her bare neck. She'd circled the campus twice after picking at her shrimp pad thai during dinner. Usually she loved Thai night in the dining hall, but ever since her bowling date with Julian, she'd been completely distracted. She'd smoked a pack of Marlboro Lights down to the last two, and now her olive-colored cashmere fingerless gloves from Barneys reeked of smoke. But she barely noticed. Her mind kept circling back on itself over and over again: *who could Julian have lost his virginity to?*

He was only a *freshman*, she thought as she trundled through the snow, purposely stepping across the lawns instead of the plowed sidewalks. It made her feel good to burn off some energy. This time last year, Julian had been an eighth grader. How do you go from the eighth grade to having sex? (Never mind – according to Heath Ferro and his wild imagination, he'd lost his virginity on a prospective weekend at Waverly. To a senior, no less.) She imagined Julian as the Dustin Hoffman character in *The Graduate*, only a lot taller and much cuter, having been seduced by some cougar next-door neighbor or friend of his parents.

Tinsley looked up to see the warm, yellow lights from the windows of Maxwell Hall welcoming her in from the cold. She clomped up the steps and ducked into the door to the mailroom.

She shook the snow from her boots and stepped around an Abercrombie & Fitch catalog covered with footprints. She stood on her tiptoes to peek into the tiny glass window of her box – empty. A pod of freshman girls giggled at the bulletin board in the far corner, sipping from their steaming coffee cups and scanning the board for who knew what. She was about to turn and leave when she thought she heard Julian's name. All the girls laughed in unison and Tinsley's heart quickened. What were they saying about him? She casually drifted toward them, taking out her phone and pretending to send a text. The girls' voices got maddeningly quieter as Tinsley approached, and the more she strained her ears, the less she could hear. The girls burst into a fit of giggles and then ripped down a flyer from the bulletin board, looking at Tinsley as they rushed out of the mailroom, the smell of peaches and strawberries and café mocha swirling in their wake.

Tinsley stared at the fresh blank spot on the bulletin board. Slivers of pink were stapled tightly around the empty spot where the flyer had been posted. For a brief, nightmarish second, she imagined the flyer reading SLUTTY GIRL STEALS JULIAN MCCAFFERTY'S V-CARD in giant block letters. She turned away from the bulletin board, feeling stupid.

She caught a glimpse of Brandon Buchanan hurrying out of the student lounge, a sleek black squash bag thrown over his shoulder. The squash team – yes! Julian and Brandon played on the team together, and everyone knew that guys bragged about their conquests in the locker room, so chances were the whole squash team would know Julian's hookup history. 'Hey!' she called out, dashing out the door after Brandon.

He gave a tentative wave in response but didn't slow down. On the steps of Maxwell, she caught up with him and placed a hand on the arm of his black down parka. 'Hey,' she said again, trying to sound natural. As if she were always going out of her way to talk to boring, metrosexual Brandon. 'What's up?'

Brandon regarded her face carefully, as if searching for a hidden agenda. 'Nothing,' he said shortly. 'Just headed back to my room to study. Why?' He stepped cautiously around an icy patch on the cement stairs.

'No reason.' Tinsley shrugged her shoulders casually, seeing her breath in the cold night air. Damn Brandon for being so suspicious. Was it so hard to believe that she was just being, you know, nice? Most Waverly guys would jump at the chance to have Tinsley Carmichael show a little interest in them. 'I'm headed your way.'

Brandon looked at her askance and then shrugged his shoulders, too. 'Whatever.' He tightened his Burberry scarf.

'Coming from practice?' Tinsley asked cheerfully, tapping Brandon's squash bag. 'Julian's always talking about squash.' The absurdity of the complete non sequitur almost made her laugh. She would have felt like a moron if she were talking to anyone except Brandon. But she knew too much about him from Callie – i.e., he actually paid extra to have the Fluff-and-Fold laundry service *iron* his boxer shorts – to be embarrassed. Tinsley squinted at a plume of smoke rising from the chimney of Dumbarton. Part of her wanted to call the whole investigation off and just curl up in front of her dorm's common room fire.

But she *had* to know whom Julian had slept with. She had to know who her competition was.

Brandon shot her a glance like she was crazy. 'Uh, yeah. He's a good player.'

He kicked at a snowbank with the toe of his impossibly shiny Kenneth Cole boots.

Tinsley glanced out the corner of her eye at Brandon as they walked down the path. Was he trying to say Julian was a *player*? Or was he merely commenting on Julian's squash skills? 'He said the same thing about you,' she said, even though it wasn't true.

'Yeah?' he said casually, but Tinsley could see him standing a little straighter at the compliment. Boys were so predictable.

Tinsley nodded. 'Yup.' She paused a moment, staring up at the fat, yellowish moon hanging in the dark sky. 'He also said that squash players get the most girls.'

Brandon stopped in his tracks and stared at Tinsley incredulously. Then, understanding dawned on him, and a self-satisfied smirk crossed his face. 'Wait, are you *checking up* on your *boyfriend*?'

'*No*.' Tinsley was forced to stop too. A couple of sopho-mores passed them on their way to the library, their arms stacked with textbooks. 'Why? Should I be?' Her wide, dark eyes focused on Brandon's face, searching for secrets.

Brandon shook his head in disbelief. 'Tinsley, I have no idea what you're up to, and frankly, I don't give a shit.' Chuckling softly to himself, he turned up the path to Richards, leaving Tinsley standing alone in the middle of the walk.

Tinsley stomped on down the path, silently wishing a rash of zits would magically appear across Brandon's well-moisturized face. Snowflakes started to fall gently from the sky, but she was too preoccupied to notice. In the distance, she spotted Wolcott, the freshman boys' dorm. Suddenly, all she wanted to do was talk to Julian. Tell him how the news that he wasn't a virgin had floored her. How she couldn't sleep without picturing him hooking up with other girls, or how she'd been so distracted this morning that she'd actually thrown on a pair of Brett's ankle boots – a size too small – and hadn't noticed until halfway through the day, when her toes had started to ache.

Then she noticed that the lights were off in the first-floor corner room. Julian must still be at the library for the mandatory algebra study session he'd been complaining about. Her heart sank.

Until she got a much better idea.

Taking a deep breath, she waltzed into the building, ignoring the gawking looks of the freshmen dorks sprawled around a coffee table playing Risk. She marched right up to Julian's room and tried the knob, knowing that Julian was too trusting ever to lock it. It opened.

Tinsley flicked on the overhead light and took in the messy room, which Julian shared with another freshman named Kevin. She'd only been here a couple of times. She had a reputation to uphold, and hanging out in a freshman dorm – regardless of how hot her boyfriend was – was unheard of. There *had* to be some kind of evidence of Julian's past love life: photographs, letters, movie ticket stubs he couldn't bear to part with. She smiled at the giant black-and-white Bob Dylan poster over his hastily made bed, the acoustic guitar hanging from a hand woven strap against the wall, the framed photograph of a five-year-old Julian frolicking in the surf with a black Lab.

But she had a purpose. Her eyes scanned the bookshelves – maybe a photo album? – and landed on a well-worn paperback called *Love Poems of the Twentieth Century*. Had it been there before? She plucked the book off the shelf and fanned through the pages, stopping at some of the underlined passages with suspicion. Maybe it was something assigned in Miss Hannaford's freshman comp class. The thought made her feel better, until she landed on a page with a tiny heart penciled in next to a W. H. Auden poem. There was no way in hell Julian would doodle a heart in a book. She quickly shoved the offending book back into its place and wildly glanced around the room, looking for more evidence.

The sleek white iMac on Julian's desk caught her attention, but she stopped herself. Casual snooping was one thing, but Tinsley wasn't about to turn into one of those girls who searched their boyfriends' computers. Besides, when she nudged the mouse, she saw it was asleep. Instead, she peered into his half-open desk drawer, which contained nothing more than a couple of pens with teeth marks on the caps, several unsharpened pencils, and a book of stamps.

She felt like an idiot. Was she really expecting to uncover some kind of incriminating evidence that would reveal whom Julian had lost his virginity to? She was grabbing the poetry book for another look when something on his desk shimmered in the corner of her eye. It was a silver foil matchbook with the name of a restaurant in New York, the Blue Water Grill. She flipped open the cover, expecting to find a woman's name scrawled inside, but the unused matches stood at attention, mocking her. Why hadn't he used any of the matches? she wondered. Was this some kind of souvenir, a memento from a special night?

'What's up?' a voice asked, and she spun around to find Julian's roommate, Kevin, standing in the doorway, a giant backpack slung over his shoulder. A red cable-knit cap with earflaps was tugged down low on his forehead.

'Hey,' Tinsley said coolly, as if Kevin were the one intruding.

He grinned goofily at her, his chin covered in small patches of stubble that refused to grow in further. Clearly, his time at Waverly had not yet taught him how to talk to females – or to properly groom. Perhaps the activities committee should offer a freshman seminar on the topic. 'What are you, uh . . . doing here?' he asked, eyeing Tinsley, still in her winter coat.

'Nothing,' she said, shrugging. She leaned against Julian's desk, trying to shield the book of poems from view. She wondered if he'd seen her handling the matchbook.

'Is Julian here?' he asked, confused, as if Julian might be hiding under the bed or in the closet. He set his backpack down on his bed, which was made with a red fleece blanket covered with smiley-faced baseballs. What was he, twelve?

'No, I don't think so. The door was just open.' Tinsley twirled a lock of hair around her still-gloved finger, and smiled shyly at Kevin. 'I was just going to leave him a note, if you don't mind.'

'Oh,' Kevin said, kicking some snow off his boots. 'Totally! I didn't mean to interrupt you.'

Tinsley smiled, satisfied. He was apologizing to *her* for

breaking into *his* room. 'Thanks. You're so sweet.' She searched for a scrap of paper on Julian's desk to leave the promised note. She picked up a pen, then paused, her brain whirring into action.

She turned around and contemplated Kevin. He was Julian's roommate. Why overlook him as a valuable source of information just because he was slightly annoying and had bad facial hair instincts? 'I haven't seen you around, Kevin. Where've you been hiding?'

'I just got back from New York,' he said, proudly. 'You know, Thanksgiving.'

'Right,' Tinsley said, putting her hands on her hips. 'I didn't see you at Yvonne Stidder's party.'

A hurt look crossed Kevin's face. 'I made you a drink,' he reminded her.

'Oh, right.' She couldn't be blamed for not remembering him. That night in Yvonne's Upper East Side penthouse, she'd been too freaked out by the appearance of Sleigh Monroe-Hill, her completely wicked former freshman roommate, to pay attention to much else. Sleigh had had a complete mental breakdown and had ended up leaving Waverly after Tinsley had hooked up with a guy she liked. To enact her revenge, at Yvonne's party Sleigh had practically thrown herself at Julian, who'd come down to New York to spend Thanksgiving with Kevin's family. But wait, how did Sleigh know Julian in the first place? He couldn't have . . . slept with *her*? 'You and Julian were hanging out with, uh . . .' Tinsley touched her forehead lightly, pretending to think. '*Sleigh*.'

Kevin nodded, flopping down on his bed and grinning up at Tinsley. He pulled off his knit hat, revealing a matted-down head of greasy blond hair. 'Yeah, she's pretty cool.'

Tinsley nodded in faux agreement, although 'pretty cool' was about the last thing she'd call Sleigh. 'How does Julian know her?' she tried to ask as casually as possible, grabbing a stack of Post-its from Kevin's desk and tearing one off.

'Oh, Sleigh's mom and my dad are partners in the same law firm in the city.' He tried to straighten the collar of his ugly plaid shirt. 'Julian didn't know her before the party at all.'

Tinsley was relieved – at least Sleigh wasn't the one who'd managed to steal Julian's innocence. But how the fuck was she ever going to find out whom Julian had slept with at this rate? Her mind whirled, trying to replay all the times she'd seen Julian talking to girls, but it seemed pointless.

An awkward silence passed and then Kevin asked, 'Do you want to, uh, hang out? I think there's a *Law & Order* marathon on tonight.' He shoved his nervous hands into his Gap jeans and got to his feet.

'That sounds totally tempting,' she lied. She scrawled a quick *Miss you* on the yellow Post-it, stuck it to Julian's computer monitor, and dropped the pen into his cluttered desk drawer. 'But I have to jet.'

'Cool,' Kevin said, crestfallen. 'I should probably, you know, study or something . . .' His voice trailed off.

'Tell Julian I stopped by, will you?' She batted her eyes at him as she breezed into the hall.

'Sure,' she heard him say. She listened for the sound of Kevin closing the door, but he left it open, and Tinsley knew he was watching her as she left.

Now, if only Julian could be as easy to read.

From: BrettMesserschmidt@waverly.edu
TO: Waverly Student Body
Date: Wednesday, December 4, 9:02 P.M.
Subject: Secret Santa (shhh!)

Hi everyone,

This is your friendly junior class prefect, officially announcing the start of the Secret Santa season! Each of you will receive a private e-mail from me momentarily, letting you know who you'll be secret-shopping for this year. A few rules: Please don't exceed the fifteen-dollar price cap. Homemade/creative gifts are welcome, and encouraged. Of course, keep it appropriate.

And the best part – reveal yourself to your Secret Santa at the Holiday Ball next Saturday at the Prescott Faculty Club. Flyer attached. Fun for everyone!!

Happy Holidays, all!

Best,

Brett Messerschmidt

From: SatansLittleHelper@hushmail.com
TO: Undisclosed recipients
Date: Wednesday, December 4, 10:16 P.M.
Subject: Secret Santa, Part 2

Calling all troublemakers:

By now, you've all gotten your Secret Santa assignments. I'm sure you're all very excited about getting a pair of Waverly Owl socks from your SS . . . but I have a better idea.

Secret Santa is lame. I say we go wild this year, and change it to Secret Satan. Let's put the fucking X back in Xmas. Leading up to the Holiday Ball, let's give each other totally crazy, against-the-rules gifts. (Our very own class prefect said to be creative!) Anything vulgar, dirty, lewd, rude, filthy, perverted, indecent, or immoral is fair game. The wilder, the better.

First rule of Secret Satan: you don't talk about Secret Satan – to anyone.

Second rule: get your freak on!

xxx,

Satan's Naughtiest Elf

8

A WAVERLY OWL IS ALWAYS OPEN TO MAKING NEW FRIENDS.

'So, tell us about yourself.' Claire Goodrich, the tallest of the three freshmen girls interviewing Jenny, spoke up. Her light brown hair was cut into a bob, and a short fringe of bangs fell awkwardly into her pale green eyes. She and the other two girls were crowded around Jenny's desk in the art studio.

When Jenny told the girls they could meet her after her Thursday afternoon painting class, they'd begged to come early and watch her 'in action'. She'd said no, not wanting to disrupt class with her little film crew. But when they pressed, she told them they could at least come a little early and watch her clean up. Now the studio had emptied out, and the three girls eyed Jenny with goofy grins on their faces.

Jenny wiped at her cheek, certain she'd left behind a splotch of burnt sienna paint.

Izzy Vanderbeek, a short brunette whose job was something she called 'blocking out the shots', blew her nose and stared at the studio's enormous plate glass windows and the towering skylight-filled ceilings. She had a cold and kept pulling tissues from a mini Kleenex pack in the pocket of her Waverly Swimming hoodie. 'This is such an awesome space.'

Kaitlin Becker, a curvy girl with glasses and orangey red curls, had one knee on the floor and was slowly tilting her sleek black Sony camcorder to take in the whole art studio before focusing on Jenny. Jenny felt the camera on her fingers as they twisted caps onto tubes of paint, and she had to admit, it made her feel kind of famous. She almost wished she'd let them film her during class, just so the other students could see.

'Make sure you get the painting, Kaitlin!' Izzy ordered, blowing her nose. 'It's really good.' Jenny glanced at her canvas, with its only half-done still life of apples and tree branches. It wasn't very good . . . yet.

'So,' Claire spoke up loudly, trying to imitate a reporter on *Access Hollywood*. Jenny had quickly discovered that the cute girl was the unspoken leader of the group. Claire sat on a stool and leaned back against a desk. A couple of forgotten brushes rolled off the edge of it and clattered to the floor. 'Jenny, is it true you almost got expelled?'

Jenny looked up at the camera and saw its unblinking

red eye staring back at her. Suddenly, she felt like she was on stage. She'd loved going to off-Broadway plays with her dad as a kid, staring up at the actors, wondering how they could possibly be so composed in front of hundreds of people. She took a deep breath, actually feeling kind of dramatic in the outfit she'd chosen especially for her first shoot: a dark red silk Badgley Mischka ruffled blouse, snatched from the clearance rack at Bloomingdale's over Thanksgiving break, and a pair of black pegged-bottom Theory trousers her dad Rufus had paid for as an apology for not telling her about his ashram having their Thanksgiving feast at their Upper West Side apartment. The outfit was partly covered by Jenny's off-white, paint-splattered smock. 'Wow, you guys don't mess around,' she said in a voice she hoped came off as coy and mysterious.

All three girls twittered in excitement. Jenny grabbed her brushes and turpentine. The camera followed her over to the giant metal sinks, and Izzy whispered instructions as Jenny poured turpentine on her brushes and scrubbed out the oil paint residue. 'What about the barn at Miller's farm burning down? Did you have anything to do with that at all?'

Jenny smiled mysteriously as if to say, *I'll never tell*. She tried not to splatter water on her blouse as she patted the brushes dry with paper towels.

'Come on, you have to give us something!' Claire squealed, pushing up the sleeves of her pale purple J.Crew button-down.

'How did you end up at Waverly in the first place? Did you really get kicked out of Constance Billard?' Kaitlin asked eagerly, sticking her head out from behind her camcorder. Her glasses sat crookedly on her freckled nose.

Jenny tossed her dark curls – which she'd treated to some of Callie's Frédéric Fekkai deep conditioning last night in preparation for her day on camera – over her shoulder. The girls followed her back to her desk, where she put her brushes away into her art bin. 'Let's just say I wasn't invited back.'

The girls looked at each other and smiled, their eyes lighting up at this bit of information.

'*Told* you,' Izzy whispered to Kaitlin, taking another swipe at her nose with a crumpled tissue. Then Izzy suggested heading over to Maxwell Hall to get some 'crowd shots'. Jenny felt her stomach flutter at the thought of people actually seeing her being followed by cameras. She zipped up her orange quilted Guess? jacket and slung her black canvas messenger bag over her shoulder.

'Is it also true that you modeled for Les Best?' Claire asked, tugging a pair of white fuzzy mittens onto her hands as the girls exited the art studio. In front of them, the afternoon sun lit up the white-blanketed Waverly campus. Students in colorful parkas and scarves rushed out of the aged brick academic buildings, eager to be released from afternoon classes. As the girls strode down the freshly shoveled walkway in the direction of Maxwell Hall, video camera rolling, Jenny kind of felt like she was starring in

a New England prep school reality show. Which she kind
of was.

'Yes, but . . .' Jenny answered, a smile spreading across
her face at the memory of her short-lived modeling career.
She and Serena van der Woodsen, her friend and total
Manhattan glamour girl, had done one shoot for the famous
designer, and it had been featured in *W* magazine. She kicked
the toe of her hunter green wellies into a clump of snow.
'I was lucky enough to be in the right place at the right
time,' she answered modestly.

Izzy eyed her. 'What was it like, then?'

Jenny loosened her striped scarf. In the distance, she saw
a clump of guys in lacrosse jackets, and she wondered if one
of them was Drew Gately, the senior she'd had an almost
disastrous flirtation with. She kind of wished it was him, so
that he could see her talking to the camera. 'I was hanging
out with Serena van der Woodsen, who was one of their
perfume models. And the designer saw us together and
somehow came up with the idea of putting us on a motor-
cycle, riding off into the sunset down this deserted beach.'
She shrugged, as if it was no big deal, but she still had a
couple of photos from the shoot at home under her bed. She'd
been shocked at how arty and elegant the black-and-white
shots had turned out. She looked natural and beautiful, even
next to Serena. Professional photographers were like an expensive pair of jeans: they made you look so effortlessly *good*.

'Excuse me.' A voice spoke out from the door to the
mailroom as the girls hurried into the foyer of Maxwell

Hall. Jenny recognized the guy who worked behind the counter in the Waverly mailroom. He had a button saying PACKAGE TOO LARGE FOR BOX pinned to his chest. 'Are you Jenny Humphrey?'

Jenny blushed, feeling the camera on her face. 'Y-yes,' she stammered, wondering how the mailroom guy knew who she was when she'd probably only picked up a handful of packages. Out of four hundred students, he remembered her? It was kind of flattering.

'Mailroom was closing, and someone left a package for you,' he said, producing a daintily wrapped box the size of an engagement ring. 'Just need you to sign for it.'

'Oh, we need to get this on camera!' Izzy nudged Kaitlin in the ribs, even though the handheld camera had been taking in the whole scene.

'I got it,' Kaitlin replied, zooming in on Jenny's face.

The mailroom guy – kind of cute, in a Nintendo-playing way – eyed the video camera curiously. Jenny signed her name with a flourish on the clipboard in his hand, pretending he'd asked for her autograph. 'Thanks,' he replied, holding on to the pen she gave him for a second too long.

'Mailroom guy totally likes her!' Claire whispered to Izzy, who leaned toward the camera screen. The tiny package Jenny held in her hand was wrapped in red paper and tied with a white bow. Her heart raced. Her first Secret Santa gift at Waverly!

'Who is it from?' Claire whispered excitedly, although there was clearly no card or label. Jenny held a corner of the ribbon in her fingers and let the package hang delicately in the air, twirling it around for all the girls to admire.

'It's from my Secret Satan.' Jenny slid the ribbon off a corner of the box, hoping it didn't contain something dirty. Ever since the mysterious 'Secret Satan' e-mail had gone out last night, Waverly students had been bombarding each other with slightly scandalous gifts. That morning, Jenny had seen Emily Jenkins open an envelope in her mailbox and pull out a pair of panties with a giant bunch of cherries printed on them. At lunch, Kara Whalen had showed her the hot pink feather duster she'd found on her doorstep, with a note that said, *For use on naked skin only.* Jenny herself had been assigned Yvonne Stidder – boring! – but hadn't gotten her anything yet.

'Don't you mean Secret *Santa?*' Claire asked innocently.

Jenny arched her eyebrow at the camera. 'Do I?'

The girls giggled and the camera shook. Jenny waited a beat for Kaitlin to steady it before she pulled off the ribbon. *Please don't be something embarrassing*, she thought to herself, recalling the sight of some skinny freshman guy walking into class with a spray can of Whipped Body Cream. She'd die if someone had gotten her something related to her boobs, like an enormous Lady Grace bra.

'What do you think it is?' Izzy asked before stepping away from the camera to blow her nose.

'Perfume, maybe?' Kaitlin guessed, sounding as nervous as if the gift were hers.

'Too small for perfume.' Claire touched her bare earlobes absentmindedly. 'Maybe earrings. Diamond ones.'

Jenny laughed. 'Somehow I doubt that.' The ribbon fell away and one of the girls surreptitiously picked it up and folded it into her pocket. Jenny opened the lid on the box, slowly, in case something awful sprang from inside.

Instead, she saw a bangle bracelet made from a thick piece of translucent coral. It was beautiful. Jenny lifted it out of the box, half-expecting a note explaining that it was actually some kind of sex toy. But the box was empty. She slid the bracelet onto her wrist.

'Ohmigod, that's like the sweetest thing in the world!' Claire exclaimed, reaching out to touch it as Jenny showed it off for the camera. 'Who could it be *from?*'

By now, the foyer had started to fill with students loading up on caffeine before heading to the library for the evening. Jenny hadn't noticed how busy Maxwell had become, but now, dozens of people were shooting curious glances her way. A cute guy in her English class, the grumpy-looking goth girl who sat across the aisle from Jenny in algebra, a couple of senior field hockey girls – they were all looking at her, seemingly impressed.

'Someone who really likes you!' Izzy squealed. 'I hope it's some hot senior.'

Jenny shook her head. She'd had enough of hot seniors after Drew. But maybe her Secret Satan could be a hot junior.

Or just hot.

'Ohmigod,' Kaitlin whispered, the camera still on Jenny.

'That totally cute exchange student from Amsterdam just gave you this *look*. Maybe it's from him.'

Was her Secret Santa out there, watching? She resisted the urge to look up, to wildly search the passing faces for the faintest hint of a knowing smile. Instead, she twisted her wrist, watching as the lights glinted against the smooth, polished surface of the bangle. A couple of girls walked by and whispered excitedly. Just another moment in Jenny Humphrey's glamorous life, she imagined them thinking. And she *did* feel glamorous, for once, enjoying the feel of her totally sweet Secret Santa bracelet on her wrist. *This is just the beginning*, she thought as she felt Kaitlin zooming in on her face.

Jenny couldn't help it. She brushed her hair back and gave the camera her most glamorous smile.

OwlNet   Instant Message Inbox

RifatJones: Found a tube of Sex Kitten colored lipstick in my box today!

EmilyJenkins: I see your lipstick and raise you a pair of cherry panties.

RifatJones: Whatever. I'm psyched to not get another Waverly lanyard this year.

AlanStGirard: Yo, my SS slipped a coupon for a full-body massage under my door.

LonBaruzza: Too bad u don't know if it's from a chick or a dude.

AlanStGirard: Shit. U just killed my buzz.

LonBaruzza: Come over here then. My little Satan gave me a mini bottle of Absolut and a martini glass.

AlanStGirard: Who u think's behind all this SS shit? Ferro?

LonBaruzza: Who else?

BennyCunningham: Fess up. Are you Satan's Little Helper?

HeathFerro: I'm not little anywhere, baby.

BennyCunningham: Sigh. U know what I mean.

HeathFerro: Don't know what u r talking about . . . but I remember there being a rule not to talk about what you're talking about.

BennyCunningham: U r nuts. And the only one dirty enough to get this started.

HeathFerro: I'm flattered!! Get any lingerie that you want to show off yet?

HeathFerro: Maybe in my room?

A WAVERLY OWL KNOWS THAT PERSISTENCE IS THE KEY TO GETTING WHAT SHE WANTS.

Callie paused at the third-floor landing of Dumbarton Hall, her legs feeling like they were filled with lead. *That's what happens when you get old*, she thought, conveniently forgetting the fact that she'd just come from the gym, where she'd spent an hour pretending to read *Vogue* on a Stair-Master. She'd actually been scoping out the gym for dateable guys, without any luck. They were all either too sweaty, too skinny, or too boring . . . or too taken. Her mind kept turning back to the image of Sebastian casually strolling into the dining hall, his dark hair falling across his forehead.

Callie paused in the hallway and stared miserably at the dry-erase board stuck to Verena Arneval's door. A note written in masculine handwriting read, *See you tonite, hottie.*

Fuck. Even Verena, with her ugly, slightly masculine short haircut, had a guy?

The door to 303 was slightly ajar, but the lights were off. 'Jenny?' she called out. Nothing. 'Hello?' She flicked on the light.

The room was empty save for a small package sloppily wrapped in newspaper, propped up on her desk, absent a bow. Callie's heart thumped excitedly in her chest. Her first Secret Satan present! *It isn't a present unless it has a bow*, her mother used to say. But hell. Now that she didn't have a boyfriend, even a crappily wrapped present made her heart race. How pathetic was that? The whole campus had been full of chatter about Secret Satan and the progressively taste-less gifts left in people's rooms, and here she was, looking forward to opening a creepy-looking package that probably contained edible condoms. (Did they even make those? Ew.) She tore into the package and turned over a small box about the size of a pack of cigarettes.

It was a deck of cards. On the front, an old lady smiled over her pince-nez glasses, her hair piled on top of her head in a towering gray bun. They were . . . *Old Maid* cards? All the excitement drained out of her and Callie felt her fingers tremble in shock and anger. What the fuck? She hurled the cards toward her trash can. She couldn't get fruit-scented oils? Glow-in-the-dark condoms? Even the naked cupid-shaped chocolates that Alison Quentin proudly showed off at lunch would have been better than a stupid deck of Old Maid cards. That was just *mean*. Besides, the gray-haired old maid on the box cover bore an eerily striking resemblance to Callie's bitchy old grandmother, who lived in West Palm Beach. All she did was play bridge with other rich, wrinkled widows, wear too much jewelry, and drink gin and tonics from noon onward.

Callie threw her gym bag to the floor and jumped into the shower, hoping the hot water would make her feel better. It didn't. As she wrapped herself in an off-white Egyptian cotton towel and stared at her bare skin and damp blond hair in the mirror, all she could think about was how hopelessly single she was. And if her Secret Satan was right, things weren't changing anytime soon . . . or ever.

Until she saw the flyer taped to the bathroom mirror from the Senior Class Activities Fund that read *Pizza + College Application Party. Seniors: Buried in college apps? Come to Reynolds Atrium on Thursday night for some pizza and company – you bring your applications, we'll bring the pizza!*

In record time, Callie threw on her clothes: a pair of wide-leg J Brand jeans and a sage-colored St John Collection fitted cashmere turtleneck that brought out the green in her hazel eyes. She sprayed some Oscar Blandi protein mist on her hair and gave it a shake. She quickly swiped her Nars eye shadow in All About Eve across her lids, grabbed her coat, and was out the door. There was no time to do any more. She was crashing the senior pizza party, and she had work to do.

Her mind raced as she walked through the dark quad toward Reynolds Atrium. The enormous contemporary structure, financed by Ryan Reynolds's father, the inventor of the soft contact lens, was lit up in the distance like a giant lighthouse. Callie pushed through the enormous revolving glass door into the warm atrium, her eyes immediately scanning the crowd for the one face she was looking for. Seniors lounged on the cushy red Pottery Barn–type couches, pages of papers spread out over the glass-topped coffee tables. The lush potted ferns and ficuses made the whole room feel green and tropical, and the smell of pizza filled the glass barrel-vaulted space.

'Hey, Cal!' Emily Jenkins sidled up to Callie, a tiny zit on her cheek covered by a mountain of concealer that only highlighted the blemish. 'Want a sip?' She offered Callie a silver flask engraved with the initials E. M. J. 'Whiskey.'

'No, thanks,' Callie declined, mildly annoyed to find Emily, also a junior, at the party. She scanned the horizon and quickly discerned that the *senior* pizza party was *full* of crashing juniors: Sage Francis and Benny Cunningham sat cross-legged on the floor, helping seniors Celine Colista and Evelyn Dahlie organize a stack of papers. All four of them drank from lidded Styrofoam cups, and Callie suspected they weren't drinking virgin hot chocolates. 'I might steal some pizza, though.' Callie drifted toward the stacks of pizza boxes in the corner, more interested in getting away from Emily than in having a greasy slice.

She hovered near the boxes, but the collective smell of pepperoni, pineapple, and onions turned her empty stomach. No one had seemed to really notice Callie's presence at all, besides Emily, who didn't count. She missed the days when she and Brett and Tinsley would take a party by storm, everyone's eyes turning to them as they sauntered through the door, fashionably late. And then when she'd been with Easy, they'd been the hottest couple on campus. Now, it was like she was invisible – an invisible old maid. She dislodged a mini can of Diet Coke from a stack on the table and took a sip.

Then she saw him. Sebastian Valenti was kicked back on one of the couches, wearing a pair of tan corduroys and a pale blue Abercrombie & Fitch button-down with the sleeves rolled to his elbows. His untouched applications were piled in front of him, serving as a coaster for his most likely spiked bottle of Gatorade. Callie felt a smile coming to her face. How had she never noticed this stunning specimen? Brett had talked about him, of course, as the guy she was tutoring, but she always seemed annoyed with him. Suddenly finding a hot guy at Waverly who wasn't burdened with a girlfriend or an unkissable face felt as completely incredible as discovering a coveted trunk show item in your size, just when you thought there were none left.

But as Celine and Evelyn – both wearing slinky tops far too sexy for a pizza party – moved over to Sebastian's couch, it became apparent that Callie wasn't the only explorer on this expedition. They slid down next to him, one on each side, like cheap game show hostesses. Celine whispered something in his ear, and Sebastian smiled and nodded, his dark, floppy hair falling across his forehead. Callie casually made her way over to them, trying to hover inconspicuously in the background.

Chandler Dean, a senior guy sprawled in an armchair, stopped talking about how he'd taken his dad's Porsche for a spin over Thanksgiving when he noticed all the girls paying attention to Sebastian. 'Dude, you haven't even started,' he snapped, nudging the foot of his John Varvatos loafer against Sebastian's stack of applications, still lying untouched on the table.

Sebastian ignored him and smiled at the ladies surrounding him. 'Anyone like another slice?' he asked politely before slipping away. The girls watched admiringly as he left.

'Isn't he *incredible*?' Evelyn Dahlie asked. With her pale, bleached blond pixie 'do and red cat's eye glasses, she looked kind of like an Icelandic pop star. Not Sebastian's taste, Callie could tell. She was a little more worried about Celine, with her perfectly smooth olive skin and perky boobs.

'I saw him first.' Benny giggled, coming up behind Callie and slinging her arm over her shoulder. 'Don't you remember, Sage? I told you I saw him studying with Brett and thought she should get on that.'

Sage furrowed her brow. 'Yeah . . . but I thought you were joking.'

'He drives a Mustang,' Evelyn added. 'How retro is that?'

Callie stared at her, wondering if she really was from Iceland or someplace where they didn't have Mustangs.

'I'll let you know,' Celine said casually, flipping her dark hair over her shoulder. Even in the dead of winter it was easy to pick Celine out of a crowd of students. Jealous freshmen spread rumors that she used a tanning booth in town, but Callie knew her father was Lebanese and guessed that was probably why she looked so good when everyone else was winter pale. He was a big-shot director and Celine always bragged about the Hollywood stars she got to lunch with over breaks. 'I told him about being an extra and he said he'd love to meet my father. Said he was going to be in LA over Christmas anyway – which may or may not be true, but who cares? – and I told him to look me up.'

'Wait,' Benny gasped, her pink-tinted mouth dropping open. 'Where did he go?'

They all turned, none too subtly, toward the food tables, but Sebastian's tall, dark figure was nowhere in sight.

'Shouldn't waste this,' Evelyn said, unscrewing the top to Sebastian's Gatorade bottle. She took a sip, then passed it to Celine.

The chatter in the room seemed to increase, and Callie touched her forehead, feeling suddenly overheated. She knew Sebastian would be back soon – he'd left his stuff here – and she needed a plan.

She decided to step outside for some fresh air. Just as she entered the revolving door, Sebastian appeared on the other side, coming back into the atrium, a package of Marlboro Reds in his hand. He smiled casually at Callie through the glass and she felt her skin get even hotter as the two of them shuffled through the glass door. In another second he'd be back in the lion's den. While Callie was only an average math student, she was smart enough to know that once Sebastian retook his seat amongst the overeager groupies, her odds would decrease dramatically. She needed to act now.

Without another thought, she pulled on the metal bar in front of her, stalling out the revolving door and causing Sebastian to crash against the glass.

'What the hell?' he asked, his voice muffled by the glass. He touched his hair reflexively, as if checking his body for bullet holes. Then he turned around and saw Callie, grabbing the metal bar and leaning away from it, anchoring the door closed.

Callie giggled. 'Hey,' she managed to say.

Sebastian sensed a game was being played, though he couldn't guess what. A slight look of confusion crossed his face, but he continued to smile at her. Even though there was a sheet of inch-thick plate glass between them, Callie could see the glint of mischief in his dark eyes. 'What are you doing, blondie?'

'I'll let you out if you have dinner with me tomorrow night,' she said boldly. She felt like a wild game hunter, snaring Sebastian in her trap.

'You know I'm stronger than you.' His muted voice filtered through, a sexy smirk on his lips. 'I could just push my way through.'

'Dinner would be more fun,' she flirted. She tilted her head slightly so that a lock of strawberry blond hair fell in front of her face.

Sebastian appraised her, his smile widening. 'Yeah, I guess it would be.'

'Pick me up at eight. Dumbarton,' she said as a late-arriving senior appeared breathlessly outside the revolving door, a 'what the fuck?' look on his face when he saw Callie and Sebastian trapped inside. 'Don't be late.'

She gave the door a push and Sebastian was spit out inside the atrium. She glanced back over her shoulder to give him a smile to show that she was serious.

The look on his face was priceless.

A WAVERLY OWL ALWAYS PLAYS BY THE RULES — AND NOT THE MADE-UP ONES.

'Watch this, Ferro,' Brandon Buchanan said sarcastically as he threw his sweaty squash practice clothes into the wooden hamper at the foot of his bed and carefully replaced the lid. 'This is what you do with dirty clothes.'

Heath lay on his back, shirtless, on his unmade bed, reading his *Dark Knight* comic book. 'Don't be such a douchebag.' He didn't even glance up at Brandon. The floor of Heath's half of the room was covered with rumpled clothing that gave off a host of offensive odors. Normally, Brandon just dealt with it, but on Friday afternoon, after a long week of the guys wisecracking about his imaginary Swedish girlfriend, all he wanted to do was relax in a clean – or at least, relatively clean – room.

With a sigh, Brandon slid into his wooden desk chair, his hair still wet from his post-practice shower. He loved the aching of muscles that only came when you gave your hardest. The team's first squash match was next week, against their rivals, St Lucius. Brandon had been so busy psyching himself up for it – and daydreaming about Hellie – that he hadn't even opened the e-mail from Brett Messerschmidt with his Secret Santa assignment. Already, the campus was abuzz with Secret Satan – there wasn't a doubt in Brandon's mind that Heath was behind it, and he was determined not to give his annoying horny roommate the satisfaction of buying anything perverted for his Secret Santa gifts. Brandon clicked open his e-mail from Brett and frowned. 'Who is Mark Frederickson?'

'Dude, you're not supposed to tell anyone who your Secret Satan is!' Heath dropped his comic book in disgust. He propped himself up on his pillow, his disheveled hair sitting on top of his head like a bad hat. He blew a kiss to the giant poster of Megan Fox in *Transformers* that hung crookedly over his bed. Brandon was forbidden to touch it – as if he wanted to.

'I love you too much to harbor any secrets,' Brandon shot back sarcastically.

'Wait, Mark Frederickson – I think I know that guy.' Heath's eyes lit up. 'He's always reading *Moby-Dick*. Takes it with him everywhere – I saw him reading it in the locker room the other day. Moby-*Dick*! You can totally fuck with him. *Nice*.'

Brandon cringed at Heath's advice. 'Everyone in Doc Gilbert's class reads *Moby-Dick*. I'm sure it's not because he *likes* it.' The last thing Brandon wanted to do was give some stranger something perverted. 'I was thinking more like a sweater or something,' Brandon replied, closing his laptop.

'Man, have some *sack*.' Heath stared at Brandon in disbelief. He swung his bare feet to the floor and sat up, scratching his bare chest. 'Get the guy some anal beads. Or what about a set of chocolate dicks from that adult candy shop in Wickam?' His green eyes widened and he held his hands in the air to indicate something huge. 'A *Moby* dick.'

'I don't know if it's a real word.' Brandon glanced out the window. Snow was falling, and under one of the gaslights on the path in front of Richardson, two people stood with their arms around each other. 'And I'm not going two towns over to buy some X-rated candy,' Brandon scoffed. Since Brandon and Heath's tryst with the Dunderdorf twins over Thanksgiving, the immediate buddy feeling of having accomplished something together had receded. Brandon had reverted to his disdainful feelings toward Heath, whose slothful qualities seemed to announce and define him wherever he went.

Heath continued to harangue him with a list of suggested gifts, each one as vile as the next.

It was too much. Brandon grabbed his black Diesel

bomber jacket from the hook on the door. 'Shut the fuck up. I'm going to buy him a fucking sweater, all right?'

He slammed the door behind him, but still managed to hear Heath shout, 'I bet he'd like a whale-shaped dildo better!'

'Look what my Secret Santa got me!' Teague Williams thundered down the hall, waving something red and lacy over his head. Brandon jumped out of the way.

Alan St Girard snatched the red thing from his hands and held it up against his flannel shirt. 'What the fuck is this?' Alan asked, fingering the lace.

'It's a cupless bra, dude.' Teague snatched it back from him and wrapped it around his neck. 'I hope she wore it first!'

Alan leaned forward and sniffed. 'Smells like chick.'

Brandon hurried out the door, the cold air feeling good against his skin. Christ – it was only the second day of this whole Secret Satan madness. Another whole week of this? He just wanted to get it over with. A glance at his watch told him the stores in Rhinecliff would still be open, and he decided to make the hike into town. Get this Mark kid a nice present and be done with it.

A light snow began to fall as he reached Main Street, and the freshly shoveled sidewalks were covered with a dusting of powder. He thought of Hellie in Switzerland and wished, for the millionth time, that she went to Waverly instead of some stupid Swiss boarding school where half the students were descended from royalty. The streetlights snapped on as Brandon stepped up from the curb, a sign he always considered good luck. Fuck Heath. The degenerate Secret Satan gifts were so childish and disgusting. Brandon knew he couldn't give this poor stranger anything remotely like that.

He headed into the antiques shop, thinking he could get Mark a classy flask or a cigarette case or something. But everything in the store was either froufrou or way over the official budget. Next he tried the used clothing store, Next-to-New, where Waverly guys bought overpriced, ironic T-shirts. But staring at the racks of clothing, he realized he didn't know what size this guy was, or anything about him. Impersonal it had to be, then. He headed back out onto the street, wishing Rhinecliff had a real downtown, with a music store or something.

As he wandered down the street and stared into the lit shop windows, he thought of the annoying annual ritual of buying a Christmas present for his father, who had no outside interests or hobbies to speak of. After years of clichéd gifts like ties and cuff links, last year Brandon had asked his father point blank, 'What kind of movies do you like? I'll buy you some DVDs.' His father's empty stare as he tried to think of a single movie was terrifying, and Brandon slunk away. A week later, an e-mail came from his father with a list of titles obviously put together by one or more of his assistants. He was sure his father had never seen *Pulp Fiction* or *Amélie*, and couldn't dissemble the plot of *Lock,*

Stock, and Two Smoking Barrels if his life depended on it. Brandon ended up giving him a silk Versace tie instead.

Brandon finally wandered into Illuminations, a small gift shop. The store was empty except for an elderly woman behind the counter, flipping through a copy of *The New Yorker*. Brandon nodded hello as he carefully made his way past a rack of greeting cards with pictures of dogs wearing different kinds of hats. The small aisles of shelves were over-stuffed with prepackaged candles and soap sets giving off enough conflicting girly scents to make him lightheaded. He lifted a small, pretty pink bottle of bubble bath and unscrewed the top. It smelled like strawberries and cream, and for a brief moment, Brandon allowed himself to imagine Hellie in a bubble bath, her long blond hair pulled up in a tangled bun.

'You open it, you buy it,' a cranky voice cried out. Brandon glanced at the old lady, who hadn't looked up from her magazine. He kept the pink bottle in one hand, thinking he'd send it to Hellie with a sexy note.

Mark Frederickson, however, was more difficult to shop for. As Brandon turned a corner, his coat brushed against a silver Christmas tree, knocking a round blue ornament to the floor. Luckily, it landed on a faded, salt-stained Oriental rug instead of the worn hardwood floor. Brandon quickly replaced the ornament. In front of him was a display of baskets with packaged smoked cheeses and meats. If Heath were here, he'd probably insist on buying the obscene-looking beef stick.

Brandon turned from the beef display in disgust and found himself in an aisle lined with candles of every color and size. What about a candle? That was a nice, innocuous gift, right? Even though they were technically forbidden in the dorms, it was always nice to light a candle if there was a girl in the room – or if you wanted to disguise the smell of a sweaty, unwashed roommate like Heath. Brandon touched a gift basket of mini candles wrapped in blue cellophane – nice, but over the fifteen-dollar budget. Instead, he grabbed a small green candle in a glass jar from the top shelf, scented cedar. He took a sniff and felt like he'd walked into a forest. A nice, impersonal scent.

The bell above the door dinged as another shopper entered and Brandon made his way to the counter, careful not to touch the Christmas tree. He wondered if he should skip dining hall food and eat at Nocturne, the diner up the road. Maybe the baked lasagna. He set the cedar candle and the pink bottle of strawberry bubble bath for Hellie on the counter and the woman rang him up. She expertly wrapped the candle in purple tissue paper and dropped it into a small brown paper bag with purple ribbon handles.

'Do you deliver?' he asked, glancing at the bag. He grabbed the bottle for Hellie and dropped it into his Hermès messenger bag, but he didn't exactly want to stroll into Nocturne carrying what was obviously a Secret Santa gift – not to mention a daintily wrapped one.

The woman nodded, pushing her glasses further up her nose.

'I'd like to send this to Mark Frederickson, at Waverly,' he said.

'Just fill out a card,' the woman said, tossing a card on the counter.

Brandon searched his pocket for a pen and the woman reluctantly produced the one clipped to the inside of her shirt. As he bent down to write Mark's name in his neatest handwriting, a flash of light sparked in the corner of his eye, distracting him. He looked out the window, but didn't see anything. He went back to the card and the flash popped again. This time he traced the source to the other shopper, a girl wrapped in a long dark coat, her camera phone pointed toward Brandon. She snapped another picture and then ducked out the door.

'What *was* that?' Brandon asked, staring out the door.

'Damn kids,' the owner said, grabbing a baseball bat next to her and looking like she was going to hop over the counter and chase the girl down. 'Instead of buying things, they take pictures of them.' She pushed up the sleeves of her sweater and shook her head again. 'I could murder the guy who invented cell phones.'

Brandon nodded in agreement, worrying about the old woman's sanity as he finished the card to Mark Frederickson. He handed the woman his American Express platinum card, paying extra for the present to be dropped off that night. He changed his mind about the baked lasagna and headed back to campus instead, happy that he'd satisfied his Secret Satan assignment in such a classy fashion.

Although part of him wished he'd bought the beef stick and stuck it under Heath's pillow.

KirinChoate: Ohmigod, just saw Brandon B buying candles and bubble bath in town.

AlisonQuentin: Maybe his Swiss GF is visiting?

KirinChoate: No, she's made up. They were for Mark Frederickson!!

AlisonQuentin: Ohhh. No wonder Sage broke up with him.

AlanStGirard: Heard u got some bubble bath for someone special?

BrandonBuchanan: What's it to u?

AlanStGirard: Nothing. Just think its sweet.

BrandonBuchanan: R u spying on me?

AlanStGirard: I heard that Mark F loves to take baths. Make sure to lather him up good.

BrandonBuchanan: WTF? The bubble bath is for Hellie, you jackass.

AlanStGirard: Thought her name was Helga? What else are you keeping from us?

A WAVERLY OWL KNOWS THAT FINDERS DOESN'T ALWAYS MEAN KEEPERS.

'I wanted the spicy tuna rolls to come with the wasabi *separately*. Not everyone wants it wrapped inside,' Brett Messerschmidt snapped into her cell phone as she trudged away from Hopkins Hall late Friday evening, her weary legs leading her in the direction of Dumbarton. She hated wasabi, and she hated even more the arrogant caterer they'd hired for the Holiday Ball. Brett had met with him twice already, and he was a fat old man who thought the only opinions that mattered were his own. 'Look, I don't care how you normally do it. This is the last time I'm having this conversation. The wasabi comes *separately* or Waverly Academy is never doing business with you again.' She snapped her phone closed, feeling a surge of power.

The Disciplinary Committee had decided that since Brett

had done such an efficient job with the Secret Santa assignments, she should take charge of the whole planning committee for the Holiday Ball – or at least, that's how they spun it. Rumors were floating around that Emily Strauss had had a mini nervous breakdown and couldn't do anything except stare at her Yale personal essay on her laptop, leaving the planning committee in the lurch.

And so Brett spent the entire afternoon with the committee, made up mostly of dorky, overachieving sophomores she didn't even know. Now her head swirled with floral arrangements and table settings. Her mouth was dry from tasting frosted cupcakes and miniature fruit tarts, and if one more florist or caterer tried to tell her she couldn't have what she wanted, Brett was going to lose it. She felt like she was planning a fucking wedding instead of a high school formal. The pride she'd initially felt about being given such a big responsibility had dissipated – any more days like this and her schoolwork would start to suffer. She would end up needing a tutor . . . like Sebastian.

Almost the second his name popped into her brain, Brett rounded the path toward Dumbarton and spotted Sebastian himself on the front steps, the cold breeze ruffling his dark, ungelled hair. He was leaning against one of the porch columns, looking incredibly uncomfortable in a slightly too-small navy blue peacoat, open at the neck to reveal a neatly pressed button-down. Brett was sure she was hallucinating, her sugar levels finally skyrocketing after too many cupcake tastings.

She stopped in her tracks at the bottom of the steps, rubbing together her tan leather gloves to warm her hands. 'I thought you were all booked up this week. You look like you're going *yachting*.'

'Yeah, well . . .' Sebastian nodded politely, tugging at the collar of his shirt. Was he wearing a sweater over it? A sweater-*vest*? 'A man's got to get some air.'

Brett narrowed her eyes at him and stepped carefully up the recently salted steps, her pointy-toed black ankle boots with the three-inch heels not exactly the best cold-weather footwear. She pulled up the collar of her Nanette Lepore emerald green jacquard coat. 'Don't tell me you miss our study sessions already?' she asked, curious. What was he *doing* here? Her toes tingled in her boots. Was he here . . . to see her? Brett had a sudden urge to invite Sebastian in for some microwaved hot cocoa in the common room.

But a strange look Brett couldn't decipher crossed Sebastian's face, and he pushed his longish hair out of his face. He opened his mouth to say something, but before he could, the front door to Dumbarton flew open, revealing Callie Vernon, buttoning up her Jill Stuart puff-sleeved crimson coat over a silky black dress and her shiny black riding boots with the four-inch heels. 'All set.' Callie grinned at Sebastian, touching her hand to his arm.

Brett froze. Sebastian was waiting for . . . *Callie*? She felt like she was in an elevator that had suddenly dropped fifty floors.

'Brett!' Callie squealed at the sight of her friend. She

rushed over to give Brett an air kiss, the scent of her Jean Patou perfume making Brett's eyes water. 'You should have seen the pretty flowers Sebastian brought me!'

'Really,' Brett said, her mouth suddenly feeling like sandpaper. 'That's very sweet of him.'

Callie's blow-dried hair and pale pink eye shadow made her look positively angelic. 'We're off to dinner now – want me to bring you something back?' she asked, hooking her arm into Sebastian's. He grinned shyly at Brett.

'I'm good, thanks.' Brett sucked in her cheeks and somehow managed to throw open the door to Dumbarton. In a flash, she remembered the look on Callie's face the other day when Sebastian walked into the dining hall wearing his new clothes. She remembered how, just last week, over strawberry piña coladas in the upstairs common room, Callie had gone into another one of her fits bemoaning the lack of eligible boys at Waverly. About how she needed someone new.

And of course, Brett remembered her childish bet with Sebastian, who was positive that if he de-greased himself, he could land any girl at Waverly.

Apparently, he was right. Starting, of course, with Brett's former BFF.

'Are you hungry?' Sebastian asked Callie softly.

Callie shrugged and pulled on a pair of cream-colored cashmere gloves. 'A little,' she answered.

'I called ahead and got us a table by the window,' he told her, raising his voice a little so that Brett could hear.

Where was he taking her? Brett wondered furiously. Le Petit Coq? She pictured the two of them in one of the cozy window nooks, watching the snow fall and sharing wine as a fire crackled in the old stone fireplace.

'Sounds perfect,' Callie said, tugging him a little toward the steps. 'We should, uh, get going.' She winked at Brett.

Brett stood on the steps, feeling like a third wheel. *He's just doing it to be an ass*, she thought to herself. *No, forget that: he* is *an ass*. If Sebastian were Cinderella, she knew he'd turn back into a pumpkin sooner or later, his hair finding its way back into a greasy mess on top of his head, his skin reeking again of Drakkar Noir. Callie might be fooled by Sebastian's metamorphosis, but Brett knew better. It served Callie right if she was desperate enough to get sucked in. *Better her than me*, Brett thought, though it took her an uncomfortably long time to convince herself of the idea.

'Have fun, kids,' Brett called over her shoulder, trying to keep the annoyance out of her voice. But she couldn't help glancing back as she opened the front door. The crisp night air tousled Callie's hair, and the almost full moon lit up Sebastian's clean-shaven face as he turned back to give Brett a grin. She let the door slam shut.

To her surprise, Brett's annoyance morphed into a stabbing jealousy. She marched through Dumbarton and slammed the door of her room, grateful that Tinsley was off somewhere. She unzipped her boots and kicked them into the corner, not caring that they were crusted with snow or that the hardwood floors would be covered with puddles soon. Wasn't *she* the one who'd spent all that time tutoring Sebastian? Inviting him to her house for Thanksgiving? Listening to Bon Jovi in his car with him? Like *Callie* was ever going to do that.

She flopped down on her Indian-print fuchsia comforter and stuffed a pillow under her head, trying to block out any memory of the conversation where she bet Sebastian that he couldn't attract Waverly girls. If he wanted to date a blue-blooded Southern belle, he could go right ahead and do it. Why the hell did she even care?

She decided she didn't want to know the answer to that question.

A WAVERLY OWL KNOWS TRUE POTENTIAL WHEN
SHE SEES IT.

'Ritoli's?' Callie Vernon asked in surprise as Sebastian's black Mustang screeched to a halt beside the pizza place in downtown Rhinecliff. Her ears were still ringing from the Bon Jovi medley Sebastian had burned onto a CD just for the short ride into town. The music was awful enough, but Callie had to stare out the window to avoid looking at the Magic 8 Ball Sebastian had somehow managed to fix to his gearshift, or the diamond-encrusted *S* hanging from the rearview mirror. (She hoped it wasn't real – what a waste of diamonds.) The inside of Sebastian's Mustang was fogged with some cheap cologne that smelled like CVS, and by the time they pulled over on Main Street she was gasping for breath. She'd kind of hoped he'd take her to Le Petit Coq, the fancy French restaurant at the edge of town, where the portions were tiny and the food was artfully arranged on white china plates.

But Ritoli's was better than the KFC off the freeway, which, after seeing Sebastian's car, wouldn't have surprised her. Ritoli's was kind of cheesy, but Waverly students loved it because they delivered late – and the girls especially loved it because the waiters were notoriously cute. Maybe some Waverly Owls would be there and see her with Sebastian. She wanted word to spread as quickly as possible that she'd claimed him.

'They've got the best garlic cheese bread this side of Sicily,' Sebastian said proudly, hopping out of his Mustang and quickly rushing over to open Callie's door. Well, that was sweet. *And* he had told her he liked her outfit – when was the last time any of the Neanderthals at Waverly had paid homage to her fashion sense? Except Brandon – and that was only because he noticed *everyone's* fashion sense.

Callie stepped carefully around a snowbank. Through the enormous windows of the restaurant, a red leather booth sat with a single candle in the center of the table. In that lighting, the pizza place did look kind of romantic.

'Sebastiano!' a voice from the kitchen cried out as Sebastian held the front door open for Callie. The smell of pepperoni hit her in the face.

'*Paisano!*' Sebastian called back, taking Callie's coat and hanging it on the coatrack. Then he slid out of his own dark peacoat – which looked brand-new – just as a large man threw his arms around Sebastian. Callie noticed a small flash of gold underneath Sebastian's baby blue Salvatore Ferragamo button-down and she stared intently. Was he wearing . . . a gold necklace? She slid uneasily into the red leather – scratch that, *vinyl* – booth, running her hands over the red and white checked tablecloth to make sure it was clean.

'What, you don't come around anymore?' A large, red-faced Italian guy approached them, his arms out. He wore a purple silk shirt partially sweated through. Callie hoped he didn't handle any of the food.

'Man, they're busting my ass to graduate.' Sebastian grinned. Callie straightened her back and took a deep breath. She didn't want to be a snob or anything, but if she and Sebastian were going to have any sort of future, he was going to have to lose expressions like 'busting my ass'. Not to mention expressing difficulty in actually graduating from Waverly. *Everyone* graduated, didn't they?

'Ah, forget about it,' the Italian said, waving his hands. 'I never even went to high school and look at me!' Sebastian hugged the guy again – were they related? She really hoped Sebastian didn't look to him for college advice.

The Italian grabbed Sebastian's face as if he might kiss him. Then he noticed Callie. 'It looks like you're pretty lucky yourself, with such a lovely companion for the evening.' Callie tried to smile brightly, but the compliment didn't do much for her from the lips of an overweight, greasy old guy. 'Enjoy, enjoy, huh?' the guy said, bowing slightly in Callie's direction as he receded back into the noisy kitchen.

'Sal is great,' Sebastian said, sliding into the bench seat opposite Callie.

'He seems . . . nice.' Callie tried not to wonder what Sal had been doing that made him sweat so much. If Callie's mother had been there, she probably would have called the health department from her cell phone.

But Callie was on a date, after all – nothing else really mattered. She wasn't sitting home, using the stupid knitting kit her bastard Secret Satan had sent her this morning. She carefully arranged herself in the booth, straightening her clingy black Calvin Klein wrap dress. Maybe she was a little overdressed for Ritoli's, but at least she knew she didn't look like an old maid. It was her first date with Sebastian, and she wanted it to lead to many future dates. She couldn't help keeping score. The car and choice of venue were against him, but he *had* showed up with flowers, even if they were the kind of gaudy red roses packaged with gobs of baby's breath they sold at the supermarket. She'd dropped them into Jenny's green Nalgene bottle and left them on her desk.

'Everything here is great,' Sebastian said seriously as he opened his oversize menu.

Callie pressed her lips together and did the same.

Or tried to – the laminated pages inside were covered with a dried splotch of red sauce, causing them to stick together. The menu made a small tearing sound as she wrestled it open, but Sebastian didn't seem to notice. He was engrossed in the list of pastas, his lips moving as he contemplated each one.

'What do you recommend?' Callie asked demurely, staring at the list of pastas swimming in various artery-clogging cheese and Alfredo sauces. Weren't Italian women supposed to be thin? What on Earth did they eat?

'My go-to is the linguini with clam sauce.' Sebastian looked up at Callie, his dark eyes alight. 'Sometimes I get it with Alfredo sauce, but the clam sauce is almost as good as my Nonna makes.' He flashed a smile, and despite Callie's recoiling at the thought of gooey Alfredo sauce – and its million calories – she found herself smiling. It was sweet that he mentioned his grandmother.

Callie glanced up at the black-and-white photograph hanging on the wall of a man in a top hat bicycling down a narrow street in Rome. 'I think I'm just going to have the tomato and mozzarella salad.'

Sebastian eyed her incredulously, his dark eyes wide with disbelief. 'Shit, are you one of those girls who only eats *salad*?'

'*No*,' Callie insisted, crossing her arms over her chest, annoyed, even though her lunch every day, and often her dinner, consisted mostly of green lettuce leaves. 'Besides, I *like* salad.'

'Yeah, right. *Rabbits* like salad.' Sebastian chuckled, leaning back in his seat.

Callie's eyes caught again on the gold chain peeking out from his shirt. Did he wear it everywhere? Or was it only for special occasions? Either way, it wasn't okay. 'So, um . . . what else do you do at school? Besides, you know, study with Brett?' she asked, desperate for something to say. She tried to remember back to other first dates – were they always this awkward? Maybe she was just out of practice? Her first 'date' with Easy, after all, had been a frantic make-out session in the rare books library during a boring party for *Absinthe*, the school literary magazine. Not exactly practical preparation for *this* – although it did make her wonder if Sebastian was a good kisser.

Sebastian narrowed his eyes at her. 'As little as possible.'

Callie laughed nervously and started to twirl a lock of her blond hair around her finger, a bad habit she had when she was distracted or anxious. Was she trying too hard to make something happen with Sebastian when there wasn't anything there? But then she remembered hearing that Evelyn Dahlie had invited him to a seniors-only party that very weekend. Probably in her bedroom, that skank. Sebastian was too cute to be available for long – and if Callie wanted a boyfriend, this was her chance.

'No, I mean, like, in your free time?' Callie leaned forward, hoping to give Sebastian a tantalizing peek at her lacy pink

La Perla camisole. She looked up at him from beneath her mascaraed lashes and gave him her most flirtatious smile. 'What sports do you play? You look like you're in great shape.' There was a mandatory PE requirement at Waverly that students satisfied by playing a fall, winter, or spring sport, so Sebastian had to play *something*.

Sebastian rubbed his chest, looking flattered. 'Ah, I play some b-ball. Nothing like a good game of pickup to get your blood flowing.'

Callie nodded politely, not sure what the hell Sebastian was talking about. Baseball? Basketball? 'That's cool.' She touched her earring nervously. Someone turned up the Italian music coming from the speaker in the corner and the sound of wailing violins made her think she was in *The Lady and the Tramp*. Which, unfortunately, made Sebastian the tramp.

Their waiter came over with a bottle of red wine she hadn't even seen Sebastian order and half-filled Callie's and Sebastian's wineglasses.

'*Cin cin*,' Sebastian announced, holding his glass up in the air. Callie raised her own glass, ignoring the water spots, and clinked it against his. She took a small sip of the wine.

'*Cin . . . cin*,' Callie repeated. Her father was half-Spanish, and she'd spent a good amount of time in Barcelona, where he'd grown up. So she half-understood Spanish, which was similar to Italian . . . so maybe that was one thing she and Sebastian had in common. Maybe his family had a place in

Italy somewhere. She imagined a picturesque Italian coastal village and a sprawling ancient villa with amazing views of the Mediterranean.

Sebastian was staring out the window at the snow-covered cars on Main Street. In the dim, orangey glow of the street-lights, she could see the snow falling, but when she caught Sebastian's eyes again, she thought she saw a bored look in them.

'You don't like the snow?' she asked, starting to panic. Sebastian was bored already? The vision of her perfect Italian villa disappeared like a soap bubble.

'Hate it.' Sebastian shook his head, his almost black hair sliding into his face. He had this kind of young Johnny Depp thing going on. 'You ever been to the shore?'

Callie wasn't sure what he was referring to. 'You mean the beach?' she asked, biting her lip. The image of the sun-sparkling blue waters of the Mediterranean instantly returned.

'The Jersey shore.' He smiled, but looked at Callie suspi-ciously, as if he could imagine what she was thinking. 'You've heard of New Jersey?' he teased.

'Tell me about it.' Callie swirled the remnants of her wine in the glass, hoping to look sophisticated. New Jersey wasn't the *worst* place to live, despite what Brett thought. He could have been from, like, Kalamazoo or something. Or Las Vegas. But before she knew it, Sebastian was detailing for her the merits of the Jersey shore, all the fun things to do there, the bars that stayed open late, the fried food available – fried dough, fried ice cream, fried onions, fried anything you wanted – the neon-lighted carnival rides and sleeping on the beach 'until the pigs chased you away'.

'Interesting,' Callie said as their young Italian waiter set down a steaming plate of pasta in front of Sebastian and a giant salad in front of her. At least it wasn't fried dough. Callie couldn't think of anything more unappealing than walking along a boardwalk crowded with tattoo parlors and arcades, the scent of fried grease drowning out the smell of the ocean.

'You'd like it there,' Sebastian said, pouring more wine in Callie's glass. He looked her in the eyes and smiled. The gold chain flashed again under his shirt and, the red wine going to her brain, Callie boldly leaned across the table toward him.

'What is that?' she asked innocently, her hand brushing against his collar. 'A necklace?' She couldn't think of any occasion in which she would find a guy in a gold necklace attractive.

Sebastian looked down and touched the gold cross proudly. 'My grandfather gave it to me the first time I ever visited my family in Italy. I never take it off.'

We'll see about that.

Callie leaned back in her chair, appraising her dinner date. Okay, he had awful taste in music, jewelry, restaurants, and vacation spots. But he was also handsome and truly sweet. Callie felt a familiar rush: the excitement of starting a new project. Sebastian was a diamond in the rough – he just needed a little polishing. *I can work with this*, she thought, watching as Sebastian twirled his fork in his plate of linguini. He was total boyfriend material.

Or he would be, with a few minor adjustments.

A WAVERLY OWL KNOWS THAT THE CAMERA'S
ALWAYS ROLLING.

Jenny could feel the warm summer wind on her skin. She licked her lips and tasted the salty air. All along the beach, bronzed boys in Abercrombie swim trunks watched as she sauntered to her towel near the lifeguard station. The waves roared in her ears and she pranced in the sand, her milky white skin miraculously tan, her dark brown hair highlighted with gold. She climbed the diving board, ready to plunge headfirst into the calm Pacific waters. *Wait – why is there a diving board at the beach?* The more she tried to concentrate on the water and the Abercrombie boys, the quicker they faded. The rapidly disintegrating scene was overtaken by the sound of murmuring, as if the clouds were whispering. Jenny snapped open her eyes to find a camera lens in her face.

Ohmigod. 'Wha . . .' Jenny trailed off. She could feel some dried spittle – she sometimes drooled as she slept – at the corners of her mouth. She quickly rubbed the back of her hand against her lips.

Kaitlin Becker's orangey red curls bounced behind the camera screen. 'Your roommate let us in!'

Jenny glanced at her clock radio, silently cursing Callie and the early morning Pilates class she'd insisted on taking after her bread-heavy date last night. She sat up, pulling her homemade quilt up to her chin and wishing she'd worn something sexier than her pink-trimmed gray flannel PJ Salvage jammies. At least they kind of hid her boobs. If the camera added ten pounds, she certainly didn't need them *there*.

Claire Goodrich, sitting in Jenny's desk chair, leaned over and lightly smacked Kaitlin with the back of her hand. 'Shh . . .' she hissed. 'Give her a chance to wake up.' Her bobbed hair was still damp from the shower and she looked perfectly put-together, in a New England preppie kind of way. She was the kind of girl who could pull off a bright yellow cable-knit sweater.

'We wanted to get your day from start to finish,' Izzy Vanderbeek explained, shrugging off her blue puffy down vest and dropping it on Callie's unmade bed. She turned to Kaitlin and barked: 'Pull back a little. You're too close.'

Kaitlin stepped back, a disappointed look on her face. Jenny touched her hair – it was always completely disheveled in the morning. But the red eye of the camera inspired her, and she tossed her brown curls over her shoulder, hoping they were falling in kind of a sexy, bed-headed way. 'Morning,' she said sleepily into the camera. *Please look sleepily cute and don't have eye crusties*, she prayed. 'What, exactly, do you want me to do?' she asked tentatively. She didn't care how 'real' they wanted to make this documentary. She wasn't about to let them watch her shower or pee.

Kaitlin swept her camera around the room. Izzy jumped to her feet. 'Just . . . walk us through what you do in the morning. You know, your routine.'

'Okaay . . .' Jenny threw the quilt off and slipped her bare feet into her ancient pink bedroom slippers. 'Normally I don't talk to anyone before I brush my teeth, so I'm sorry if my conversation skills aren't up to par.' Jenny grabbed her blue plastic shower caddy and headed toward the door, the freshmen girls trailing after her into the third-floor bathroom. It was empty – not surprising at this hour on a Saturday morning. Most of the other girls were still sleeping after Friday nights filled with pizza and illicit drinking.

Jenny reached for her toothpaste. She heard one of the girls note the brand, Tom's of Maine, in a reverent mumble. Another mumble of approval as Jenny squeezed some of the minty goop onto her Hello Kitty toothbrush. She held the toothbrush under the running water to erode the pile of toothpaste by half, knowing that a giant glob of toothpaste on her pajama shirt was not exactly glamorous behavior. She didn't want it immortalized on film for generations to come.

Jenny tried to make brushing her teeth look interesting, but there was only so much she could do beyond staring at herself in the mirror and raising her eyebrows.

'Get her shampoo,' Izzy directed as Jenny kept brushing. As Kaitlin trained the camera on Jenny's shower caddy, Jenny took the opportunity to spit into the sink, relieved that the camera hadn't caught that. At least her teeth were clean. Did they really want to make a film about the beauty products she used? Jenny felt a surge of panic that her ratty blue toothbrush and her Clearasil pore-cleansing pads would make her look very uncool. But she took a deep breath and squirted a dollop of Burt's Bees Orange Essence face wash into her hands. She rubbed it into her face as the camera zoomed back in and she thanked God she'd plucked her eyebrows the night before. And put away her box of Tampax Ultra.

'Soooo . . .' Claire said cheerfully as she leaned against the toilet stall and eyed Jenny. 'We know you've hooked up with lots of hot guys on campus,' she prompted in a gossipy tone. 'Like Easy Walsh.'

'And Julian McCafferty,' Izzy jumped in, her blue eyes wide. 'He's in my English class, and he's sooo hot.'

'So tell us,' Claire prodded, her bobbed hair moving in time. Jenny felt a rush of pride. This was much more interesting than her facial routine . . . but who was going to see the video? Should she really talk about something so . . . private? 'What was that like?' Claire's eyes widened expectantly.

Jenny smiled modestly for the camera. 'There are certain details a lady can never divulge,' she said slowly, dabbing her face with a rosemary-water-soaked cotton ball. The three girls looked crestfallen and Kaitlin lowered the camera a little, disappointed. The old panic Jenny felt to please everyone in the room reared. The tooth brushing had almost put them to sleep – the least she could do was give them something interesting. After all, they had chosen her, Jenny Humphrey, to be the subject of their film project. They could have asked *anyone* – but they wanted *her* story.

Jenny tucked a brown curl behind her ear and slowly answered. 'But . . . I can say . . . my fling with Julian *was* really kind of intense.' The girls giggled excitedly and Kaitlin trained the camera on Jenny again. Jenny felt like she was on stage, and she desperately wanted to wow her audience.

In reality, the few times she'd kissed Julian – wonderful as they had been at the time – had slowly faded from her memory, but that wasn't exactly dramatic enough. She tried to imagine what Tinsley or Callie or Brett would say. 'He's a *great* kisser,' she added, leaning toward the mirror and smiling at her image conspiratorially. The freshmen girls cooed.

Unfortunately, they weren't the only ones listening. Tinsley stood in the hallway, shower caddy in hand. Not willing to wait at the third-floor bathroom for a free shower stall, she'd thrown her tissue-soft Calvin Klein robe over her skimpy Cosabella jammies and headed upstairs to use her old bathroom. She'd paused at the door when she'd heard voices.

When she heard the words 'My fling with Julian was really intense . . . He's a *great* kisser,' she almost let her shower caddy clatter to the floor. Even though Tinsley had been snooping around all week, trying to figure out whom Julian had slept with, she realized now that she wasn't ready to hear it. Especially not from the unmistakable voice of cute-as-a-button Jenny Humphrey.

Intense? Jenny? Was it possible that she'd actually . . . slept with Julian?

All of a sudden, the past month of friendship – when she'd more or less forgiven that wannabe for stumbling into Waverly and stealing all her thunder – disappeared from Tinsley's mind. Gone were all memories of her and Jenny and Callie, bonding in the upstairs common room over popcorn and margaritas and bad movies, or late-night gabfests over pizza and Diet Coke. Why had she ever been fooled by Jenny's sugar-sweet attitude and sparkling, innocent brown eyes?

She stole Easy Walsh from Callie practically her first week on campus, and then she'd taken Julian. And deflowered him. That bitch.

Tinsley's eyes burned with anger as she pushed open the door to find Jenny staring at herself in the mirror, three dorky freshmen scattered around her. She'd forgotten about the freshman fan club.

'Good morning!' Jenny smiled cheerfully. Her cheeks

were flushed and her whole face looked dewy. Tinsley eyed the three girls crowded around Jenny as if she were a Greek deity or something. Jenny was really letting these losers film her in those cutesy pajamas? Was she mentally defective?

'Is this a bathroom, or *The Hills: Prep School Years?*' Tinsley asked, her voice dripping with sarcasm. The girls tittered uncomfortably. The one with orange hair in pigtails that stuck straight out from her head spun around and fixed her camera on Tinsley.

'Oh, sorry.' Jenny's warm brown eyes widened. She just looked so sweet and innocent it made Tinsley want to puke. For a second, it was hard to believe that this girl, in her gray pajamas covered in tiny rosebuds, had actually slept with Julian. Could she have jumped to conclusions too quickly? 'We were just sort of . . . filming.'

But then Tinsley remembered how she'd first found out Jenny and Julian were hooking up. Julian *had* been hooking up with Tinsley at the time, and she'd thought all was well and good between them – until, at the Cinephiles party at the Miller farm, she'd come across Jenny and Julian, sitting on a tree stump, kissing tenderly. It all came back to her like a lightning flash, and Tinsley felt her legs wobble. What had she been thinking, trusting Jenny after she'd stolen Julian from her once already? She was a serial boyfriend-stealer – and she'd managed to steal Julian's *virginity*, too.

'I'm not an idiot. I can see that.' Tinsley threw her towel

over the top of one of the curtain rods. 'But I'm taking a shower. If you don't want a lawsuit on your hands, you can turn the fucking camera off.' The orange-haired Pippi Longstocking quickly clicked off the camera and looked about ready to wet her pants.

Tinsley threw her bathrobe and pajamas onto the hook on the ceramic-tiled wall and tugged the shower curtain closed behind her. Instead of waiting for the water to heat up, she stepped directly into the freezing spray, hoping to calm down a little. But all she could think about was how Julian – sweet, sexy Julian – had cared enough about stupid little ho-bag Jenny to actually waste his V-card on her.

'Wow,' Jenny said brightly, once the sound of running water filled the bathroom. 'Someone must have had a bad night.' But her insides were shaking. She couldn't believe how rude Tinsley had been. Even if Tinsley *did* have a really bad night . . . it didn't mean she could be so insulting to Jenny. And in front of people. People with a video camera.

While in the past, she might have crumbled in the face of Tinsley's bitchy cruelty, Jenny was not about to take this lying down. She'd show Tinsley Carmichael exactly what she was made of.

EmilyJenkins: Did u see Jenny and her film crew today? So cute!

AlisonQuentin: Totally. I kinda want some freshmen to worship me.

EmilyJenkins: Think they do her laundry?

AlisonQuentin: Speaking of. My SS sent me a pack of Days of the Week thongs.

EmilyJenkins: U wearing them?

AlisonQuentin: Got Saturday written all over me!

A WAVERLY OWL KNOWS THAT A GIFT IS JUST A GIFT.

'Can we sneak into the Cinephiles screening room and watch a movie tonight?' Julian murmured into Tinsley's ear on Sunday afternoon. They were sitting on his dorm room bed, Julian's hands on Tinsley's shoulders as he massaged them. She'd pulled a muscle that morning when she'd gone to the gym and tried to work out her murderous energy by kickboxing. Some kind of jazzy music Tinsley didn't recognize was playing on his Harman Kardon stereo, and outside, the sun was starting to set, filling the room with the last of its dying rays. It would have been romantic, but all she could think about was Jenny and Julian. Julian and Jenny. Had they done it in this room? On this bed? To this music?

'Huh?' Tinsley said, shaking the horrible images from

her brain. This had to stop. She knew she was being childish
– whatever Julian had done in the past didn't involve her,
and that was just the way it was. She needed to get over
it. 'The screening room?'

'You remember it?' Julian teased, giving her shoulders
a gentle squeeze. 'Let's put something romantic on the screen
and . . .' he trailed off.

Tinsley felt the smile coming back to her face. *Okay*, she
told herself, pep-talk style. *Let's just get back to where we were
earlier this week.* She closed her eyes and enjoyed the feel of
Julian's hands on her shoulders. 'And do what?' she
prompted, in a husky voice.

Julian leaned forward, his breath close to her ear. Tinsley
suddenly felt warm in her black Free People sweaterdress
and she leaned back against Julian. He was about to answer
when there was a knock on the door.

Julian kissed her neck softly, sending shivers through
her whole body, before standing up and opening the door.
No one was there, but on the floor was a small package,
neatly wrapped in paper. 'Looks like my Secret Satan was
here,' Julian said with a smirk, tossing the red package on
his desk.

'You're not going to open it?' Tinsley asked, suddenly
suspicious. What was Julian trying to hide? Tinsley certainly
wouldn't have been afraid to show him her gifts – not that
they were anything to write home about. Everyone had been
getting super-dirty things, but all Tinsley had was a bottle
of olive oil – she didn't even want to think about that one

– and a gift card to a music store. Just plain random. What was Julian hiding?

Julian shrugged and grabbed the box. 'Sure.' Okay, maybe he wasn't hiding anything, Tinsley thought guiltily. She glanced over his shoulder as he unwrapped the package and pulled out a DVD.

'What is it? *Girls Gone Wild*?' Tinsley laughed.

Julian flipped the DVD over and Tinsley's mouth dropped when she saw *To Have and Have Not*, one of the most romantic movies of all time. 'Cool.' Julian pried the plastic covering off it, oblivious to Tinsley's discomfort. It was one of her favorite movies – you could practically *see* Humphrey Bogart and Lauren Bacall fall in love on-screen.

Tinsley snatched the movie from Julian's hands and flipped it over, staring miserably at the black-and-white photographs on the back. This was ten thousand times worse than any stupid soft-core porn – this was actually a thoughtful gift, bought by someone who wanted to give Julian something he'd really like. From someone who really *liked* him.

Or loved him. The room started to spin and Tinsley's tongue felt heavy in her mouth, as if she'd just done a shot of Goldschläger.

'I've actually never seen it.' Julian leaned against the back of his wooden chair and crossed his arms over his chest. He had on a faded blue long-sleeve T-shirt that read ELLIOTT

BAY BOOK COMPANY, and he raised an eyebrow flirtatiously. 'Wanna go to the screening room and watch it?'

But Tinsley was already on her feet, sliding her shaking feet back into her black crocheted Uggs. She had to get out of there. She needed some fresh air and a chance to calm down. 'I can't. I've, uh, got an Italian test tomorrow.' Completely rattled, Tinsley touched her lips to Julian's cheek for a quick kiss before slipping on her coat. She hurried off before he could say another word.

Tinsley rushed past a flock of freshmen in the boys' front lounge, one of them holding up a pair of handcuffs lined with pink fur. She hardly noticed – she couldn't think about anything but who could have given Julian *To Have and Have Not*. She knew it was silly, and maybe masochistic of her, but the name she kept coming back to as she stomped across campus was *Jenny*. She'd *had* Julian – in more ways than one, apparently – and now she didn't. But maybe she wanted him back? Tinsley leaned down and scooped up a handful of snow. She packed it into a tight ball and hurled it in the direction of Dumbarton. It exploded against a first-floor window.

'Did you just throw a *snowball* at the window?' Callie asked lazily as Tinsley stomped through the front door. She was curled up in one of the Dumbarton common room's oversize leather armchairs, her fuzzy peach cashmere blanket wrapped up around her.

'No,' Tinsley lied, stamping the snow off her boots onto

the mat in the foyer. Angelica Pardee, their recently separated dorm parent, had instituted a mandatory Sunday afternoon common area cleaning hour, when all the girls had to pick up the thumbed-through copies of *Cosmopolitan* and *Vogue*, assorted abandoned textbooks, crumpled potato chip bags, and empty Diet Sprite cans that had collected in the common room over the week. It was annoying, but at least now the slate blue room was spotless.

On the velvety navy couch, Jenny was sprawled out with a pink plaid flannel blanket across her legs. Her dark hair was falling in loose curls framing her face, and she looked tiny in an oversize Waverly sweatshirt. At the other end of the couch sat Brett, who nodded her head at Tinsley.

Jenny smiled shyly at Tinsley, as if afraid Tinsley would lash out at her again like she'd done in the bathroom. 'We're watching *When Harry Met Sally*. Come join us.' Jenny grabbed the remote and paused the movie – an undeniably sweet gesture.

But it was also 'sweet' of *someone* to give Julian a copy of *To Have and Have Not*. Jenny certainly could have had someone drop it off at Julian's room. While hanging out with Jenny was just about the last thing Tinsley felt like doing right now, she was savvy enough to know that maybe this was just the opportunity she needed. ''Kay,' Tinsley replied hesitantly. She left her boots at the door and plopped onto an empty couch, tucking her legs up beneath her.

A miniature illustrated copy of the Kama Sutra sat on the coffee table. Tinsley's eyes widened as she saw it. 'Whose is that?' It was open to a drawing of two naked people doing what looked like some kind of handstand.

'Rifat got it in her box today.' Callie giggled, pulling her blanket up to her chin. 'Check out page seventy-eight.'

'I'm so tired of everyone being so perverted,' Brett fumed, shaking her head. Her fire-red hair bobbed furiously around her face as she crossed her arms over her chest. Jenny had finally told Brett – who had been totally on edge for the past week organizing the Holiday Ball – about the noxious Secret Satan e-mail goading everyone into buying dirty gifts for their secret person. 'I've seen like five people carrying around candies shaped like penises.'

'I haven't given Ryan Reynolds anything nearly that interesting. He's perverted enough already.' Tinsley yawned, stretching out on her sofa like a cat. She grabbed the buttercream chenille throw on the back of the couch and wrapped it around her legs. 'What about you, Jenny? Who do you have?'

Jenny bristled, sensing that Tinsley was somehow planning an ambush. She'd been so rude the other morning in the bathroom – now she wanted to know who Jenny was giving gifts to? Why, so she could make fun of her for that, too? If Jenny told her she had dorky Yvonne Stidder – who she'd overheard in the dining hall yesterday complaining about the boring jar of bath salts she'd gotten – she'd never hear the end of it. 'There's a reason they call it *Secret* Santa, you know,' Jenny joked, trying to keep the annoyance out of her voice.

Tinsley's violet eyes narrowed, and Jenny felt her pulse quicken. She definitely didn't want to return to the early days of their relationship, when Tinsley was always on the verge of strangling her. 'But look what I got today,' Jenny quickly added, tilting her head back and forth to show off the tiny, Victorian-looking barrettes with green crystal dragon-flies at the tips.

'Wow.' Brett leaned forward to examine the barrettes that held back Jenny's loose braids. 'Pretty. At least one person on campus isn't a pervert.'

'And I also got a little set of Philosophy shampoos and bath gel – in Caramel Mocha Latte and Café au Lait. Smell my hair.' Jenny leaned toward Brett, who sniffed and gave the thumbs-up.

Big deal, Tinsley thought. So she smelled like a fucking coffeehouse. But inside she seethed. How come Jenny – and Julian – were both getting sweet, thoughtful gifts and all *she* was getting was olive oil?

Callie took a giant sip from the oversize bottle of Evian and wiped her mouth with the back of her hand. 'All I got was a pair of knitting needles. And a framed photograph of an orange tabby cat with a pink scarf around its neck.' Callie made a face. ''Cause I'm an old maid, apparently.'

'I forgot, T – someone dropped this off for you.' Brett

lifted a lumpy package and tossed it over to Tinsley. It was wrapped in white tissue paper and covered in hearts.

'Thanks,' Tinsley answered, feeling the package. It was kind of weird that she and Brett were being nice to each other recently, but it was also a relief. When they'd first been forced to live together in their small first-floor room, it had been positively torture, and each had gone out of her way to annoy the other. But so much time had passed that now the feuding-roommate act was hard to keep up. Tinsley had thought she'd been angry at Brett for letting her get expelled from Waverly after the E incident the June before, and Brett had been mad at her for . . . what again? Eric Dalton, the super-hot teacher who'd tried to sleep with them both? That seemed like *lifetimes* ago.

'What is it?' Callie asked eagerly as Tinsley tore into the package. She tossed the cheesy wrapping paper to the floor and unfolded a white T-shirt. The cheaply ironed-on design read *Virginia Is for Lovers*, with a heart inside a jagged outline of the state of Virginia. Tinsley blinked her eyes. *What?*

Suddenly, it was the last clue in the puzzle. Extra-*virgin* olive oil, the gift card to *Virgin* Megastore. *Virgin*-ia? Her seemingly random gifts were about her being a virgin?! Someone was definitely fucking with her. She crumbled the T-shirt up in a ball and chucked it at Callie, who ducked out of the way. 'My Secret Satan is making fun of me for being a virgin? What a jerk.'

'I don't get it,' Brett cried, clenching her hair in her fists. 'This disgustingness has to stop. I'm going to kill this Secret Satan asshole.'

'Virgin jokes seem kind of mean, even for a Secret Satan.' Callie frowned at Tinsley as she wrapped her cashmere blanket tighter around her. Still, knowing that someone was making fun of Tinsley made Callie feel better about her own lame presents – all of which were making fun of her for being single. (At least she wasn't going to be an old *virgin* maid. So that was one thing going for her.)

'What happened to presents like gift certificates to the snack bar? Candy?' Brett exclaimed, running her hands through her fire engine red hair with exasperation. Her normally perfect porcelain skin was dark under her eyes, and she had a tiny outbreak of pimples along her hairline, something that only happened to her during finals or other super-stressful times. Callie and Jenny had had to practically twist her arm to get her to chill out and watch a movie. 'The non-dirty kind, I mean.'

'Alan St Girard got a box of chocolate-covered gummy penises,' Tinsley spoke up, examining her dark hair for nonexistent split ends. 'And Verena gave her person a little box of X-rated candy hearts that say things like "Eat Me" and "Bite My—"'

'That's enough!' Brett pressed her hands, with their chewed-down blue nails, to her ears. 'Marymount's going to blame *me* when he finds out how filthy everyone's being. I just don't get it.'

'Don't worry. He won't find out.' Jenny soothed, patting her friend on the knee.

'Whatever.' Callie pulled up her blanket and stuck out her ankle. 'Who needs a good Secret Santa when you have a cute *guy* to give you presents?' Around her bare foot hung a gold chain anklet with a dangling heart charm, something Sebastian had given her that afternoon when they'd gone for a walk in the snow. It was . . . sweet. She normally didn't wear gold – or gold-plated – jewelry, and the anklet was a little tacky, sure. But it had been a while since a guy had given her something. The promise ring from Easy that she'd lost in New York didn't count – it was the beginning of the end.

This, on the other hand, felt like the start of something.

'Where did that come from?' Brett asked, her voice sounding strained.

'Sebastian,' Callie purred. The more she looked at the little charm anklet – she hadn't worn an anklet in ten years – the more it grew on her. Kind of like Sebastian. 'He's just such a sweetheart. I can tell he's going to be the best boyfriend ever.' Her hazel eyes glazed over as she pictured the two of them, exquisitely dressed, walking into the Holiday Ball together, heads turning enviously in their direction.

Now Tinsley and Jenny's glances met across the room, Tinsley stifling a snicker. 'Have you even *kissed* him yet?' she asked incredulously, pulling her glossy brown-black hair back and twisting it up in a bun.

Callie narrowed her eyes. 'No,' she admitted, biting her lip. For some reason, Brett felt a surge of relief wash over her. 'But only because he's such a *gentleman*.'

'Are we talking about the same Sebastian?' Brett couldn't help blurting out. 'The one who keeps a framed photograph of Madonna on his dashboard?'

Callie stuck her lip out petulantly. '*Like a Prayer*'s his favorite album. Well, besides everything by Bon Jovi and Springsteen.' As Tinsley and Jenny giggled, Brett suddenly felt worse. Callie had known Sebastian for about a week – and she was already bonding with him over Madonna? She didn't even *like* Madonna. And what the hell was Callie thinking, anyway? Like the governor of Georgia would ever approve of her dating a guy whose idea of high art was a sixty-inch plasma screen television?

Why did Brett even care who the hell Sebastian hung out with, anyway? Probably because he thought he knew everything. His arrogant words – 'throw a polo shirt on me and all the girls in this place will be clawing each other to get at me' – kept coming back to her, like a track stuck on repeat.

Stop it, she told herself. Brett knew she was losing it. She was just completely overloaded with responsibilities right now: she was trying to finish her final paper on *Anna Karenina* for her world lit class, finals were next week, and she'd barely cracked a book, instead having to field calls from the holiday ball DJ – who wanted to know if his friends could come to the party – and the florists, who kept running out of any flowers that weren't poinsettias. And then there was this whole Secret Santa mess that was threatening to spiral out of control.

'Whooooo!' a voice hooted as the front door flew open. A gust of cold blew into the room along with Benny Cunningham, in a calf-length camel-hair coat, and Sage Francis, a baby blue knit cap pulled down over her ears. Benny waved around a clear bottle filled with an electric green liquid. 'Absinthe!' she squealed. 'Sweet, right? Who wants a swig?'

Brett rolled her eyes. Benny was the editor of the Waverly literary magazine, *Absinthe*. At least she had a creative Secret Santa – although liquor also fell into the 'inappropriate' column.

'And I just got this!' Sage held out a black leather riding crop. She held the vile bondage toy up and set off down the hallway, chasing a giggling Benny and tracking snow all over the newly cleaned hardwood floors.

It was enough to send Brett over the edge. 'What the *fuck* is wrong with everyone?' She jumped up from the couch, nearly tripping over her fur-lined slippers. 'I've got to get back to work.'

'But we're just getting to the part where Meg Ryan fakes an orgasm in the diner!' Jenny cried out, giggling. 'Stay for that.'

Brett was too annoyed with life to respond. As she stormed back to her room, she realized one good thing had come out of her assigning everyone their Secret Santas — she'd forgotten to include herself.

OwlNet

From: BriannaMesserschmidt@elle.com
TO: BrettMesserschmidt@waverly.edu
Date: Tuesday, December 10, 10:31 A.M.
Subject: Here comes Santa Claus . . .

B,

I know you're busy with your party planning and finals and all, but I get worried when I don't hear from you.

Willy says hi . . . and hopes your friend Sebastian will spend some time at the house over Christmas break — he says to tell him he's been practicing his Grand Theft Auto and plans to kick his ass.

Write soon, li'l sis.

xoxoxo

Bree

P.S. I'm attaching a jpeg of the hot new Stella McCartney clutch that I snatched from the new samples today. I'm FedExing it to you for an early Xmas present!

15

A WAVERLY OWL STAYS OUT OF TROUBLE WITH THE LAW.

Brandon had to struggle to pay attention to Doc Gilbert's droning voice in the overheated classroom on Tuesday morning. The English teacher's chalk squeaked loudly across the chalkboard as he scratched out a discussion question from *Middlemarch*. The hissing radiators and the hot, steamy air didn't make it any easier to focus. For the past couple of days, all of Waverly had been abuzz with stupid Secret Santa – er, Secret *Satan*. Someone had given Benny Cunningham a ferret, which was just plain disgusting, with a red bow on its head. Even though pets of any kind were prohibited in the Waverly handbook, Benny had taken to carrying the ratlike animal around in her tan leather Fendi bag like she was Paris fucking Hilton. Lon Baruzza had gotten a gift bag of edible massage oils left on his doorstep, and had spent the last week personally offering full-body rubs to every single girl on campus.

Brandon felt a tap on his shoulder and glanced behind him to see Sage Francis. She wore a red ribbed Polo turtleneck, her corn silk blond hair pulled up in a tight ponytail. Her small hand held out a note for him. Two weeks ago, Sage passing him a note – combined with her sweet-smelling pear shampoo – would have sent his heart into near arrhythmia. But after she'd so heartlessly dumped him the day before Thanksgiving break, telling him he was too *feminine* for her, Brandon had fallen hard for Hellie and tried to erase all fond memories of Sage from his brain.

'Uh, okay,' he muttered, grabbing the note and ignoring Sage's wink. He unfolded the rhombus-shaped note without curiosity, and recognized Sage's loopy script handwriting: *How's your Swedish girlfriend?*

Totally jealous, Brandon thought triumphantly, as he turned around and flashed a thumbs-up sign. He crossed out *Swedish* and wrote *Swiss* in its place and tossed the note back to Sage, who giggled as she read it.

'What's so funny, Miss Francis?' Doc Gilbert demanded, throwing his chalk down on his desk in disgust. He was a short, red-faced Santa Claus–like figure – if Santa had a really short fuse and a predilection for hard liquor.

'Nothing,' Sage answered nervously, twirling the end of her ponytail around her finger. The sleeves of her turtleneck were pushed up around her elbows, and her whole face was pink, either from the attention or the near-tropical steaminess of the classroom.

'If you're not interested in learning today, Miss Francis, I suggest you leave.' The whole class quieted down and eyed the door, wondering if Doc Gilbert was actually expecting Sage to get up and leave. He made the 'suggestion' to someone at least once a week, but no one had ever taken him up on it. Brandon would have loved to watch Sage slink out of the room, but just then, the oak door to the classroom opened and a deliveryman in a brown jacket and matching brown pants poked his head in.

'Is this Weston, room twelve?' He stared at his clipboard, a slightly annoyed look on his face.

'Yes, but . . .' Doc Gilbert crossed his arms in front of his chest. 'Deliveries are supposed to go to the main office, not the individual classrooms.'

'I've got a case of wine for . . .' The deliveryman glanced back at his paperwork. 'For Julia DeSimone?' He pushed in a dolly with a giant wooden crate that read FRAGILE in block letters.

Julia DeSimone, a gangly junior with dyed black hair in the theater club, raised her hand eagerly. The rest of the class turned to look at her, unable to control their laughter. 'Right here!' she cried.

'Wine?' Doc Gilbert stepped forward, all his annoyance evaporating from his voice. 'For an underage student? I don't think so. Better bring that crate up here and I'll take care of it.' Shrugging his shoulders, the deliveryman quickly wheeled his dolly over to Doc Gilbert's desk and dumped the crate on the floor. Brandon could practically see Doc salivating at the thought of curling up with all that alcohol. 'I'll have to turn this over to the administration, I suppose.'

'Like *that's* ever going to happen,' Heath whispered loudly. Brandon rolled his eyes.

'Back to work, you overprivileged little freeloaders.' Doc Gilbert's favored way of motivating his students was by insulting them, but it was only occasionally effective. He scratched a few more discussion questions on the board but kept glancing at the crate next to his desk. Even Brandon started to wonder if it contained the $5.99 crap or the good stuff.

The door had hardly shut when it clicked open again. '*Now* what?' Doc Gilbert shouted, tossing his chalk across the room, narrowly missing Kirin Choate's head. The entire class turned around to find a police officer, his hands on his hips, surveying the room. Immediately, everyone sat up straighter in their seats, and Brandon felt himself smoothing out his collar. Had it been one of the out-of-shape Waverly security officers, in their cranberry-colored uniforms, no one would have moved, but a real police officer? A hush fell.

'Can I help you?' Doc Gilbert asked meekly. He briefly glanced toward Kirin Choate, as if he expected to be arrested for throwing chalk. He folded his guilty chalk-covered hands behind his back and stood in front of the case of wine, as if to shield it from the officer's view.

'Is Brandon Buchanan here?' the cop asked sternly, his steely blue eyes scanning the room as if comparing all their faces to a description of a suspect.

Brandon felt a sweat break out on his forehead as all eyes turned in his direction. His mind raced through the short list of things he'd ever done wrong in his life – breaking into the field house with Callie to make out on the mats, taking a hit from Alan St Girard's enormous bong one night, throwing out Heath's black Ben Sherman T-shirt he'd worn eight times and refused to wash, insisting it was good luck. But they'd either happened ages ago, or weren't exactly illegal. And then he thought of Mr Dunderdorf. Had the old man somehow discovered that Brandon had defiled his daughter and turned to the police?

'I'm Brandon.' Brandon spoke up, trying to sound brave in front of everyone. Maybe if Dunderdorf had called the cops and Brandon got sent to jail, at least then fucking Sage would believe him about Hellie. 'What did I do?'

The class was completely silent, and even Doc Gilbert seemed to be frozen in place.

'Brandon Buchanan?' the cop repeated, gripping the black nightstick attached to his belt. 'Can I see some ID?'

Benny's ferret peeked out over the edge of her purse, but she nudged it back inside as the cop stood over Brandon's desk, smelling like cheap cologne. Brandon tried to keep his fingers from trembling as he pulled his student ID card from his butter-soft Gucci leather wallet. The cop looked at it for half a second before dropping it back on the desk. 'Brandon Buchanan, you're under arrest—'

'What?' Brandon's jaw dropped, and several of the girls in class – Sage included – gasped audibly.

'For being *too damn hot*,' the cop continued, and before anyone could react, he tugged at his uniform top and the sound of Velcro ripping filled the room. The class's shock quickly turned to glee when they realized they were not actually in the presence of law enforcement . . . but rather, a stripper!

'Boo-yah!' Teague Williams whooped, clapping his hands together. Before Brandon knew what was happening, the whole class was clapping in unison as the cop – Brandon could see there was a fake-looking gold badge over his naked chest that read OFFICER BOOTY – tugged his shirt open more and touched his tanned, perfectly sculpted, and hair-free pecs.

Doc Gilbert pounded his fist against his desk to call the class to attention, but even he knew it was futile. The entire class was staring – partly horrified, partly fascinated – at the stripper, who was now strolling up and down Brandon's aisle and swiveling his hips. Brandon clenched his fists together. He'd never actually punched anyone before, but now he couldn't wait for the chance to connect his fist with the face of his asshole Secret Santa.

When Officer Booty touched his polished brass belt buckle, Brandon felt like he was going to faint. His mind swirled through all the various humiliations of his life, but nothing came even remotely close to his Secret Santa sending a male stripper to serenade him in the middle of math class.

16

A WAVERLY OWL TAKES INITIATIVE.

On Wednesday after dinner, Callie strode up the steps to Baxter Hall, the upper-class boys' dorm on the north edge of campus where Sebastian lived. It was kind of strange to walk into a boys' dorm to visit anyone other than Easy. As she stood outside Sebastian's door in the oak-paneled hallway, she caught the faint whiff of marijuana and Febreze, which made her think of Easy even more. He and Alan had always kept a stash of Febreze ready in their closet to spray down their entire room after a joint-smoking session, and sometimes they overdid it, drenching the room in the too-clean scent.

But that was over. Easy Walsh was gone, for better or for worse, and it was time Callie moved on. One of her mother's favorite platitudes — and she had many — was

'Treading water doesn't get you anywhere. You have to swim.'

And so Callie rapped her gloved hand against the oak door of Sebastian's room, right above his New Jersey Nets sticker – was that baseball or basketball? She should probably care. She took a deep breath and tried not to think about how their date had ended the other night. Sebastian had walked her up the front steps of Dumbarton, and she'd stood there stupidly, waiting for a kiss, until she finally realized it wasn't going to happen. Although she'd bragged to everyone about what a gentleman he was, it kind of weirded her out that he hadn't kissed her. Didn't he find her attractive?

Her bruised ego might have been the end of their burgeoning relationship, but the next day, he'd given her the anklet. Definitely a gentleman, despite his poor taste in jewelry.

Callie heard the soft pulse of music with a heavy bass coming from inside, so she knew someone was home. She knocked again, louder. 'Who's there?' a deep voice called out. Callie stepped closer to the door, feeling somewhat ridiculous shouting her name down the hallway.

'Callie.' The door finally swung open and Callie grinned at the sight of Sebastian, yawning, his tousled black hair falling sexily across his forehead. In his tissue-thin white Hanes T-shirt and dark wash True Religion jeans, he looked devastatingly sexy. In a kind of bad-boy way.

'Oh, hey,' he said, squinting, his eyes slightly reddened.

The faint smell of Old Spice deodorant tickled Callie's nose and she sneezed. 'God bless,' he said. 'Are you getting sick?'

Callie rubbed her nose and shook her head. 'I don't think so.' She waited a beat, rubbing her hands up and down the arms of her white bell-sleeved Tahari coat. Sebastian didn't say anything. 'Aren't you going to invite me in?' she asked, running the toe of her buckled Stuart Weitzman ankle boot against the door frame.

'Oh. Uh, sure.' Sebastian stepped aside, waving his arm graciously. 'Kind of a mess.'

Callie stepped carefully into the room. The floor was absent the crumpled clothing, abandoned notebooks, and empty Cheetos bags that always littered Easy's room. It was a nice start, but unfortunately, what the room had in cleanliness, it was lacking in décor. The only light on was a red Chinese lantern hanging from the ceiling, a tear in the paper shade letting a ray of light escape. On the wall over one bed – Sebastian's, she assumed – was a giant green, white, and red Italian flag. A red curtain was duct-taped haphazardly over the window, which was wide open to let out the smoke.

'Whoa!' Callie cried, stepping on something that squeaked beneath her feet. For a moment, she thought it was a live animal, like Benny's squirmy little ferret. But then she bent over and picked up a Nerf football. 'Cool,' she said unenthusiastically.

'Sorry,' he apologized, tossing the football into the closet. 'Blinds went missing some time after Halloween,' he said when he caught her looking at the curtain. 'Too many people climbing in and out of the window.'

Nothing a girlfriend couldn't fix, Callie told herself. 'Where's your roommate?' she asked, changing the subject. She thought she remembered that he roomed with Drew Gately.

'Don't know, don't care,' Sebastian replied, perching on the edge of his paper-cluttered desk. Were those his college applications? Callie squinted at the top one, hoping to see Princeton or Dartmouth, but it was for somewhere called Eastern Apache University, which sounded made-up. Next to the stack, a cigar box lay open with a glass ashtray inside, filled to the brim with ashes. He picked up a half-smoked Marlboro and offered it up to Callie.

Callie shook her head. An open closet door caught her eye. 'Is this your closet?' Callie asked, tugging on the sleeve of a charcoal gray John Varvatos V-neck sweater that would have set off Sebastian's skin tone perfectly. She imagined pressing her cheek to his cashmere-covered chest.

'Nah. That's mine.' Sebastian nodded his head toward the other closet, the one filled with rows of plain white Hanes T-shirts – at least they were hung up – and lots of Tommy Hilfiger. She recognized the button-down he'd worn to dinner the other night, and the handful of nice clothes she'd seen him wear over the past week, but they were sandwiched between all kinds of shiny tracksuits.

'Oh.' Callie shrugged, glancing back at Drew's closet

longingly. Maybe she could burn all the Tommy Hilfiger and Sebastian would have to start all over. 'I just think it's really sexy when guys wear sweaters.'

'Yeah?' Sebastian asked skeptically.

'I almost forgot!' Callie exclaimed, though she hadn't forgotten at all. She dug through her Fendi tote and pulled out a small box wrapped in silver paper. She held it out to him, purposefully brushing her hand against his.

'Are you my Secret Satan?' He flipped the box over and held it to his ear, shaking it gently.

'No.' She shrugged casually. But in reality, she'd always loved giving her boyfriends things. Easy would always get annoyed when she'd try to shower him with sweet little presents, and it really hurt her feelings. Sebastian, she sensed, was more laid back, less militantly anti-materialist and more open – she hoped – to being influenced by her style. 'It's just an early Christmas present.'

Sebastian tore through the wrapping paper like a five-year-old, the delicate white bow falling to the floor. He opened the box inside and pulled out the bottle of Polo Double Black. He moved it back and forth under his nose, though Callie knew that the lit cigarette in his hand probably obscured the scent.

'Are you saying I stink?' he asked, raising a dark eyebrow at her.

'*No.*' Callie tilted her head and stuck out her tongue. She stepped closer to him, letting her knee, in her charcoal pin-striped tights, brush against his leg. She was glad she'd worn her black pleated Michael Kors miniskirt. 'But I think it smells incredibly sexy.'

Sebastian grinned, his smile spreading lazily across his full lips. 'Thanks.' He set the box down on his desk, where Callie knew it was in danger of residing for the rest of the semester. Damn it. Maybe she'd actually have to spray it on him. He stubbed out his cigarette, almost knocking over his stack of applications.

That was it. She wasn't going to wait for another chance. 'Here's how you can thank me.' She planted her still-gloved hand on Sebastian's neck, pulling him toward her before he could say or do anything else. Their knees bumped and she touched her lips to his, enjoying the familiar softness of a guy's lips against hers. Sebastian tensed up for a second, but she slid her fingers up through his hair, and he started to kiss her back. The smoky taste of his mouth felt forbidden . . . and delicious.

'Wow.' Sebastian finally pulled back, looking a little dazed. He steadied himself against his desk, knocking over the bottle of Polo Black.

'Mmm,' Callie murmured, bursting with renewed confidence after the kiss. She brushed off a piece of fluff on his shoulder, her eyes landing on his hideous gold cross. She pulled off her gloves and casually reached her hands behind his neck. Before he knew what was happening, she unclasped the necklace and pulled it off him, dropping it soundlessly to his desk. 'You have a sexy neck. You shouldn't hide it with jewelry.' She touched her fingertips gently to the side of his neck, letting them linger.

Sebastian just stared at her, a slightly hazy look in his eyes, like he was still mesmerized by her boldness.

She could get used to that look.

17

A WISE OWL KNOWS THAT THE MOST OBVIOUS SUSPECT IS NOT ALWAYS THE GUILTY ONE.

'Heard you got handcuffed by a real stud yesterday, dude!' Brian Atherton snickered as he let the door to the boys' locker room clatter behind him. Running a hand across his shaved head, the senior boy smiled gleefully, probably grateful for any way to get back at Brandon for crushing him in straight sets yesterday.

'Don't worry, I gave him your number.' Brandon pushed past Atherton, his sleek black squash bag thrown over his shoulder. It was about the billionth stupid comment someone had made to him since the cop/stripper pulled off his clothes in Doc Gilbert's class yesterday. Brandon was still smoldering from the humiliation of his Secret Satan present – after the guy took his shirt off, Doc Gilbert had started shouting about calling in the real police. But the man wouldn't leave until he'd finished his routine, much to the delight of the classroom and the horror of Brandon.

The locker room's smell of BO immediately smacked him in the face. He stepped over a pile of dirty towels — couldn't these Neanderthals even put them in the bin like they were supposed to? Then another scent caught his attention, a mix of cedar and a spice that always reminded Brandon of Indian food. It was the unmistakable odor of Heath Ferro's deodorant, a brand one of his soccer teammates had passed along to him before he graduated, insisting on the almost supernatural effect it had on female olfactory senses. Brandon scoured the row of lockers for the source of the smell.

He'd waited up for Heath most of the night, lying in bed, staring at the ceiling, thinking of the best way to murder his roommate, who he now held firmly responsible for the stripper fiasco. But there was a rumor that Pierre Hausler, their dorm parent, was at his parents' anniversary party, and so Heath took the opportunity to stay out all night. Brandon had to settle for tearing up Heath's favorite Superman T-shirt, already full of holes from overuse. The satisfaction was short-lived.

Brandon spotted Heath alone at the end of the last row of lockers, sitting on a wooden bench and pulling on a red long-sleeve T-shirt. He marched toward him, his blood rushing to his face. Brandon felt like he might beat Heath to death with his racquet. The male stripper's words, *You're under arrest . . . for being too damn hot*, were still in Brandon's ears, as were the chants of *Take it off!* that had echoed around the classroom. No one else at Waverly was enough of a jackass to do something like send a male stripper to humiliate Brandon. Just like the whole Secret Satan thing, the stripper had Heath Ferro's unmistakable odor all over it.

Heath glanced up. He tugged down his shirt, his freshly showered hair pasted to his head. 'S'up, dude?' Heath stuffed his crumpled gym clothes into his Adidas bag.

Brandon's breath began to quicken. 'Where were you last night?' he asked, the question barely a gulped whisper.

Heath grinned and stood up, pulling his olive green North Face fleece out of his locker. 'A gentleman never tells,' he said coyly.

'I totally know it was you,' Brandon accused him, trying to ignore the smell coming from Heath's ancient gym shoes. He seriously hoped his mother would buy him a new pair for Christmas, at least for Brandon's sake. 'Only you would do something so stupid.'

'What are you talking about, Buchanan?' Heath looked confused. He slammed his metal locker shut with a *clank*. Brandon heard guys' echoed laughter in the showers. 'Someone put Vicks in your jockstrap again?'

'You *know* what I'm talking about.' Brandon dropped his squash racket to the floor. He couldn't imagine actually punching Heath – or anyone – but his hands kind of twitched, like they might do it on their own.

'Dude, seriously.' Heath held his hands up in the air and

widened his green eyes, the picture of innocence. Except that Brandon had seen him use that look before, to get out of everything from skipping class to making out with someone else's girlfriend. 'I have no idea.'

'You're telling me you didn't send me a male stripper?' Brandon asked incredulously. Please. Heath probably had spent his whole Waverly life fantasizing about sending Brandon a male stripper to humiliate him – the Secret Satan thing was the perfect opportunity for him. 'It was you. Don't try to deny it.'

'It wasn't me,' Heath protested, the pitch of his voice rising slightly.

Brandon narrowed his eyes. 'You're lying.'

A dark cloud came over Heath's face as he reached down for his canvas Diesel messenger bag. 'I promise it wasn't me,' he said desperately. 'Look. I got *Tinsley*.' He pulled out his iPhone and thumbed through his e-mail, scrolling until he found one from Brett. 'See.' He flashed Brett's e-mail to Heath, and Brandon saw that Tinsley Carmichael was indeed his draw for Secret Santa. 'I've been sending her all kinds of great shit.' Heath touched his hair. 'You satisfied?'

Brandon's breathing slowed as he let his squash bag fall to the tile floor. He didn't know what to think. The e-mail looked real enough, but if Heath didn't send him the stripper, then who the fuck did?

'Don't get me wrong – it was a brilliant stunt.' Heath chuckled to himself as he pulled on his fleece. 'I really wish I *had* done it. That would be fucking legendary.'

Brandon collapsed onto the bench, suddenly feeling exhausted. With Heath, it would just have been another gay joke in another long line of unfunny gay jokes. But if it was someone else, someone who didn't even know him, who had sent him a male stripper – well, that meant . . .

Brandon refused to think about what that meant.

BrandonBuchanan: Did u send me a stripper?

AlanStGirard: I just woke up, dude. Your SS got u a stripper? Sweeeet.

BrandonBuchanan: Male.

AlanStGirard: Oh, that sucks. Guess your SS thought you were into it?

From: NancyHorniman@waverly.edu
TO: BrettMesserschmidt@waverly.edu
CC: GeraldWilde@waverly.edu
Date: Thursday, December 12, 9:01 A.M.
Subject: Secret Santa disaster!!!

Brett,

The administration doesn't know who is behind the so-called
Secret Satan movement that is spreading like a disease, but
we need you, as junior class prefect and organizer of the
Holiday Ball, to get it under control. Can you do that for us?

We need everything to go off without a hitch at the party.
You'll be interested to know that Waverly alum Bethany
Kephardt will be attending. Bethany happens to be the assistant
director of admissions at Brown University – and also a former
junior class prefect at Waverly. I'm quite sure you'll want to
impress her.

We've been busy dealing with the alumni side of the ball and
are counting on you to take care of the student side.

Best,

N. H.

18

WHEN NO ONE WILL LISTEN, SOMETIMES AN OWL HAS TO SHOUT.

Brett nearly crashed into Alison Quentin as she breezed into the dining hall at lunch on Thursday, sending Alison's stack of Saltines tipping over on her tray. 'Sorry,' Brett mumbled under her breath, her tired head down as she made her way to the food line. Horniman's e-mail looped through her mind, especially the line about the Brown alum. Brett had always gotten straight A's – but so did most of the people applying to the Ivies. She'd always counted on her extracurriculars to make her stand out, but if she couldn't do her duty as junior class prefect, she couldn't exactly count on glowing recommendations from the faculty.

Brett grabbed a tray from the stack even though she felt sick to her stomach. She opted for a bowl of Special K with strawberries and a banana over the offerings of jerk chicken and lentil-barley soup. Idly she wondered if she was eating too many carbs, if that was what was sapping her strength lately. Her phone buzzed in the pocket of her TSE cardigan, but when she saw it was from the cupcake caterer, she clicked ignore.

She sank down at the first empty table she found, surprised not to find Tinsley, Callie, or Jenny anywhere. She glanced at the antique watch her grandmother had given her last Christmas: dinner was almost over. She rubbed her tired eyes.

'Hey, smell this,' someone said. Brett looked up and saw Ryan Reynolds in front of the Coke machine, blasting his neck with a fine mist of something that smelled like horse sweat.

'Get away from me.' Evelyn Dahlie pushed him away. 'It smells like vomit.'

'No, really.' Ryan chased after her, stretching out his neck for her to sniff. 'It's called something like Spanish fly. I got it from my Secret Satan, and it's like a world-famous aphrodisiac.' He laughed and hitched his thumbs in the belt loops of his black jeans. 'Or are you afraid you won't be able to control yourself?'

'No.' Evelyn stalked away, unamused. As her platinum blond hair faded into the crowd, Brett noticed Sage Francis gently whipping everyone who walked by her table with a leather riding crop. A freshman at the table in the corner where the art kids sat ate with one hand locked in a pair of fur-lined handcuffs, the free cuff clinking against the

table whenever he lowered his fork. A couple of seniors on
the swim team were playing with an enormous, superhero-size
purple dildo.

Brett pushed her tray away. Heath Ferro *had* to be behind
all this – no one else at Waverly had such a filthy mind.
But even if he had sent a stupid e-mail encouraging people
to act like nymphomaniacs, why did everyone have to listen?
There was always some random dirty guy who insisted on
slipping his Secret Santa massage oil or something, but this
was absolutely ridiculous. Where the hell was Heath,
anyway? She could kill him for turning the whole Secret
Santa operation on its head, jeopardizing her getting into
Brown.

Brett spotted the nasty-looking ferret poking its head
out of Benny Cunningham's purse across the room. Its beady
black eyes were glued to a silver glittery ring-shaped thing
that Alan St Girard was twirling into the air. Brett heard
the words 'penis pump' just as Emily Jenkins pulled something out of her pocket that looked like underwear made
from a fruit roll-up. Brett felt her heart beating faster in
her chest. Normally, she wouldn't give a shit if the entire
student body had decided to alleviate all its pent-up sexual
frustration by passing around dirty Secret Santa gifts. But
why did it have to happen this year? When *she* was in
charge?

'Full house!'

Brett glanced over her shoulder and saw Teague Williams
laying down a winning hand at the table next to Brett's.

She squinted at the backs of the cards and saw they were decorated with images of naked women of all shapes and sizes. Brett got to her feet, planning to barge over there and confiscate all the cards. Being the junior class prefect had to have *some* perks.

'Another hand!' someone cried. In the corner of the room, what looked like a deformed beach ball bounced up high in the air, but as it descended it was clear someone had blown up a magnum-size condom. Cheers went up as the condom was batted from table to table, the dining hall workers stopping their various chores to watch the impromptu game of condom volleyball.

Brett forgot about the cards, and before she could think about what she was doing, she scrambled up onto her chair. Her legs quivered with anger and she prayed it would hold. *'Everyone calm the fuck down!'* she screamed.

Instantly, the room quieted to a hush and the inflated condom hit the floor and bounced twice before rolling under a table. All eyes were on her – including the beady ones of Benny's ferret. 'This has *got* to stop!' She paused to clear her throat, remembering from her debate team days that timing was everything if you wanted people to listen. Her eyes scanned the half-empty dining hall. 'This string of inappropriate gift-giving is childish, and it needs to end now.

'The Holiday Ball is this weekend, and anyone who misbehaves will be punished accordingly. The DC will be enforcing the rules to the letter. And if you think I'm kidding, just try me!' She glared threateningly at the crowd, then carefully jumped down from her chair, grabbed her nearly untouched tray, and marched toward the tray return. As she stomped out of the dining hall, lips set in a straight line, she glanced out of the corners of her eyes. Teague Williams was gathering the X-rated playing cards and stuffing them into his pocket. Someone had popped the condom balloon with a fork, and Sage was zipping her riding crop into her backpack, looking shamefaced. Brett nodded to Sage as she walked toward the door, a hush following her as she pushed her way through the heavy double doors.

That's better, she thought, though it wasn't until she was out in the crisp wintry air that she wondered when she'd become such a cranky old lady.

19

A WAVERLY OWL KNOWS THAT THERE'S ALWAYS
ANOTHER IT GIRL WAITING IN THE WINGS.

'Beautiful,' Kaitlin Becker whispered on Thursday afternoon, crouching down on one knee. Her camera was pointed upward toward Jenny, who carefully arranged herself in the window seat of her Dumbarton room. Jenny propped one leg up as she leaned out the open window, a lit cigarette – borrowed from Callie's pack of Marlboro Lights – dangling from her finger-tips. She rarely smoked, but after an entire week of one failed photo op after another, she needed something to calm her nerves. She blew a funnel of smoke into the cold afternoon air, trying to keep it out of the room. The sun was starting to set and she hoped the last light framed her nicely for Kaitlin. In her black cowl-neck Banana Republic sweater and faded boot-cut jeans with the holes in her knees and paint splotches everywhere, she hoped she looked cute and sort of artsy – and not just boring.

Jenny had always imagined that being in the public eye was like a second skin, that after a while you wouldn't even realize that other people were always looking at you. (How else could you possibly explain all those horrible pictures of celebrities without their underwear on?) But the reverse had been true for the last week, ever since Jenny had agreed to be the subject of the freshman film class documentary: she was acutely aware of the camera's eye on her at all times. Jenny felt constantly on guard. She'd started planning things to say out in her head before saying them, knowing that they could be recorded for all time. (Or at least until Kaitlin or Claire or Izzy deleted them.) The stress had made her lose about three pounds – so far, the only really good thing to come out of it.

'Tell us about the Cinephiles party, where the barn burned down,' Claire prodded, leaning her head against the wall.

Again? Jenny wanted to ask. She swore she'd already told them about it – but her head was spinning. She'd never talked about herself so much in her life and it was starting to make her feel like a complete narcissist. But the girls apparently wanted to hear it, so Jenny did her best to recall the Cinephiles party – which felt like months ago. Was it?

Across the room, Callie was sitting at her desk in a pink spaghetti-strap Calvin Klein tank top, her iPod earbuds stuffed firmly into her ears. Her blue sparkly fingernails clicked against the keyboard of her laptop as she typed an e-mail. Jenny felt an intense longing to be e-mailing her dad instead of talking to her freshman filmmakers.

That morning, she'd had to make the three of them pinky swear to erase some embarrassing footage of her talking about how hard it was for her to buy a bra in her size. Izzy had asked her, half-jokingly, what kind of underwear she wore, and before Jenny knew it, she was railing about how hard it was to find cute bras that fit her massive boobs. Only after Claire goaded her into holding up a few of her bras for them did Jenny remember that her classmates might actually watch the film. And that maybe she didn't want them all to see her thick-strapped, unsexy double-D-cup granny bras.

Having the film crew trio following her around made Jenny realize how boring her life really was. The girls had filmed her during an art class, but they kept asking her if she could move a little more as she painted, or paint a little faster. 'Like this, or something,' Izzy suggested, grabbing the brush from Jenny and making cartoonish sweeping motions with her arm, accidentally adding a dash of red to Jenny's still life.

'And then the whole thing went up in flames . . .' Jenny trailed off, unable to think of anything else to say about the barn. She didn't want to get into the whole story about Drew, the hot senior who'd lied to her about bribing Mrs Miller to get Jenny out of trouble for the barn. All the girls wanted to hear about, though, was boys. They kept encouraging her to flirt with guys on camera, and so Jenny found herself striking up conversations with people she didn't even like – just so they could see, as they called it, an 'It girl in action'.

'But I don't get it,' Izzy said, running her hands through her short, pixie hair. Its chlorine smell was starting to drive Jenny crazy. 'Why did you confess to burning the barn down if you didn't do it?'

'I don't know.' Jenny shrugged her shoulders and glanced out the window longingly. She saw Heath Ferro and Alan St Girard pelting each other with snowballs. She wished she were out there, actually having fun, instead of sitting here and trying to make her life sound more interesting than it was.

The girls stared at Jenny blankly a minute before Kaitlin lowered the camera. She nodded her head, her orangey red curls bouncing, toward Callie, who'd abandoned her laptop and was fumbling around her closet floor. 'Wasn't *Callie* at the Cinephiles party too?'

Izzy's blue eyes lit up and Jenny stubbed out her cigarette in an empty Diet Coke can. 'Weren't she and Easy Walsh actually in the barn when it started to burn?' Izzy whispered loudly.

'I can hear you, you know,' Callie muttered, fumbling through the shoes on the floor of her cluttered closet. 'And I don't have time to be interviewed, thank you very much.'

'Where are you going?' Claire asked, and Kaitlin spun the camera toward Callie. Jenny felt like she'd been slapped in the face. Their movie was supposed to be about *her*.

Jenny knew that Callie Vernon was a way more interesting subject, but *they* weren't supposed to know that.

Callie certainly looked glamorous in her skin-toned corseted camisole and her tight-fitting black pencil skirt. She held one open-toed crimson Manolo in her hand. Her strawberry blond hair was freshly blow-dried, and she looked like a half-dressed model backstage at a runway show. 'I can't find this goddamn . . .' She trailed off, throwing expensive designer shoe after expensive designer shoe into the middle of the room. Claire hopped out of the way of a deadly stiletto. 'Aha!' Callie finally cried triumphantly, holding the matching Manolo up over her head.

Kaitlin, Izzy, and Claire giggled. A wave of panic crashed over Jenny and she crawled out of the window seat. 'Where are you going tonight, Callie?' Claire asked, and Jenny saw Kaitlin press the zoom button as she scanned the pile of shoes on the floor that Callie carelessly kicked out of her way. It was like Callie was a full-size Barbie doll.

'Huh?' Callie glanced at the girls as if she were seeing them for the first time, although Jenny had introduced them about three times now. 'Out,' she said, stepping into the Manolo pumps and stalking over to her dresser. She spritzed her wrists with her almost empty bottle of perfume and rubbed them behind her earlobes.

'With who?' Izzy asked shyly. She was sitting cross-legged on Jenny's bed, and Jenny resisted the urge to tell her to put her feet on the floor.

Callie turned toward the girls, eyeing them up and down, oblivious to the camera. A slow smile crept over her face, and she turned back to the mirror. She grabbed a silver tube of her Givenchy lipstick and ran it across her lips.

'What color lipstick is that?' Claire asked eagerly.

'Illicit Raspberry,' Callie answered, popping the top back on it and tossing it casually aside. Jenny's heart thumped in her chest at the sound of the girls cooing with interest – that was what they were supposed to do when *she* did or said something interesting.

At that moment, a Raves song started playing through Jenny's iPod docking station.

Izzy nodded her head. 'Great song.'

'I saw them in concert when I was in Madrid once,' Callie said offhandedly, mascara wand in hand. Jenny's jaw dropped. The Raves were *her* claim to fame. Through a miraculous stroke of luck, Jenny's poet brother, Dan, had temporarily joined the New York–based band as its singer/songwriter. Jenny had tagged along with them to shows, and they'd been totally sweet and charming to her.

'Really?' Claire asked excitedly.

Kaitlin zoomed in on Callie as she chattered on about the double encore and how she'd managed to get backstage with her Spanish model friend, who was a friend of a friend of the lead singer, Damian Polk.

'That's so cool,' Izzy gushed. 'I would die if I met him.'

'He *was* hot,' Callie admitted, affixing her earrings. 'He

smelled like chocolate. I always think of him when I drink hot chocolate.' Callie giggled like a schoolgirl and the camera ate it up, as did Claire and Izzy and Kaitlin.

A rising panic seized Jenny, and her mind raced for a way to bring the attention back around to her. *She* was the star of this show, after all. 'That's so funny. Didn't I ever tell you about the time I spent with the Raves?' she blurted out, trying to sound blasé about it. 'At the Plaza Hotel? And Damian's West Village town house?'

Kaitlin swung the camera around instinctively.

'No fucking way!' Claire squealed, immediately stopping in mid–dance step. 'How did you score that?' The admiration was back in her voice, and Jenny felt relief flood through her body.

'Long story . . . but I actually ended up recording a song with them.' The girls crowded around Jenny, begging her to tell them the whole story. She was so excited to have something interesting to talk about again that she didn't even notice Callie rolling her eyes in the background, having heard the story more than once.

Before she knew what she was doing, Jenny reached for her Razr. She found Damian Polk's number in her address book – she couldn't remember the last time she'd actually talked to him, but he'd insisted she could call him at any time – and let it ring, staring straight into the camera as the phone rang in her ear. The freshmen were drawing small, shallow collective breaths and even Callie stopped what she was doing to watch.

''Ello, 'ello, 'ello,' Damian answered. He sounded like he was in a long tunnel.

'Damian?' Jenny asked louder than she needed to. She'd totally expected his voice mail to pick up and hadn't planned on actually *talking* to him. She just needed to prove she had his number. She dug her bare toes into her shaggy pink rug and prayed.

'Who is this?' Damian asked.

'It's little Jenny Humphrey, silly,' she said, as if they talked on the phone every day. Her brain reeled, trying to come up with some believable excuse for calling him. Telling him she wanted to impress some freshmen girls making a movie wouldn't cut it.

After the briefest of pauses, Damian replied, his voice warm and surprised. 'Hey, cutie. What're you up to? Aren't you . . . at school somewhere?'

Jenny said a silent prayer of thanks that Damian remembered at least that much about her. 'I'm up here at boarding school in Rhinecliff.' Then her eyes landed on the embossed silver invitation thumbtacked smack-dab in the middle of her bulletin board. 'And everyone wants the Raves to play the Christmas ball!'

'Oh yeah?' Damian asked, chuckling. 'When is it?'

'This Saturday.' Jenny somehow managed to wink at the camera even though she felt like her insides were melting with panic. 'Don't say you can't come,' she teased, amazed at her own forwardness. 'We're all, like, dying up here without any good music.'

A loud static burst in her ear and she worried that the connection was lost. But Damian's voice came through the static. 'We have a show that evening, babe. Sorry.'

'We'll be out really late, though. Can't you come when you're done?' Jenny closed her eyes. 'Please, please, please?'

Damian laughed. 'I guess we can come after our show.'

'I knew you'd come through!' Jenny squealed, and Izzy, Claire, and Kaitlin all gasped collectively. Even Callie raised her eyebrows as if impressed. 'You guys rock!'

The static buzzed again and this time the line went dead. But Jenny casually closed her phone. 'It's on,' she said into the camera. 'They'll do it.' She smiled smugly as the freshmen jumped up and down.

'A Raves exclusive!' Claire exclaimed, pressing the back of her hand to her forehead as if she was about to faint. 'The coolest.'

'Does he even know where the school is?' Callie asked skeptically, pulling a translucent pink top on over her camisole.

Jenny narrowed her eyes. 'Ever heard of GPS?' she answered back. The girls tittered, and Jenny leaned back against the window and lit up another one of Callie's cigarettes – this time in triumph.

A WISE OWL KNOWS THAT THE FIRST TIME'S NOT
ALWAYS THE CHARM.

'Looks like someone got another Secret Satan prezzie!' Benny Cunningham trilled as she and Tinsley paused in front of Tinsley's first-floor dorm room. A tiny package wrapped in pink construction paper sat in front of her door, a giant T. C. written in black marker on one corner.

'Whatever. I'm already tired of this.' Tinsley kicked it with her toe. She was simply not in the mood for any more shit. A DVD of some D-list movie called *Virgin Territory* had been shipped to her from Amazon the day before, and she'd thrown it into the lost-and-found box in the mailroom.

'Not all of us have hot young freshmen to keep us entertained.' Benny wrinkled her nose and tossed the hot pink boa she'd taken to wearing – a gift from her Secret Satan

– over her shoulder. At least she wasn't carrying around the fucking rat she'd been given. She'd decided the weather was too icy today and Thumper the ferret needed to stay home.

Tinsley unlocked her door and soccer-kicked the box inside. She dropped her bag and sat on the edge of her bed, her muscles twitching. She kept hoping she'd stumble onto her Secret Santa leaving her one of the mean-spirited presents, but no luck. It *had* to be a guy – no girl would be bitchy enough to tease Tinsley about her virginity. She couldn't wait until the Holiday Ball, when everyone outed themselves to their Secret Santas – and she murdered hers.

She hoisted the package into her lap and tore into it. The pink cover of a book peeked out at her. She flipped it over and saw the title in big black letters: *The Everything But Guide: For Girls Who Won't Go All the Way but Want to Do Everything But*. On the cover was a photo of a girl who looked disturbingly like Tinsley, grabbing at her clothes as if to ward off some sort of sexual attacker.

She threw the book against the wall, where it crashed into her framed photo of Plaza San Marco in Venice and fell to the floor. Enough was enough. She was sick of being worked up about the stupid virgin gifts. Why the hell did she care so much? It was stupid to let this bother her . . . but maybe it was even stupider to let herself be vulnerable to this sort of torture.

There's an easy solution to that, she thought to herself, grabbing up her coat and marching out the door. She tromped off to Julian's room, the idea of sleeping with Julian picking up steam. Why the hell not? She'd wanted to for so long — maybe this was just the push she needed to take the plunge. Besides, they were going to do it eventually. Why not do it now and get it over with?

Tinsley pushed into Julian's room without knocking. He jumped up from his bed, where he'd clearly been napping. 'Oh, hey!' His face lit up at the sight of her. 'You scared the shit out of me.' A copy of *The Remains of the Day*, required reading in freshman English, lay facedown on his pillow.

'Where's Kevin?' Tinsley asked breathlessly, unzipping her down-filled Juicy Couture army jacket.

'His parents took him to dinner,' Julian answered, standing up and stretching his arms over his head. His Grateful Dead shirt rose up, revealing a strip of toned stomach.

'Good.' Tinsley reached over and locked the door, then leaned her back against it, enjoying the look of surprise on Julian's face.

Julian took a step toward her. 'And to what do I owe the honor of your presence?' His slow, crooked smile spread across his face, deepening the dimple beneath the left corner of his lips. Tinsley's knees went weak.

'Let's just call it your lucky day,' she said softly. She slid her arms out of her jacket first, letting it fall to the floor, then pulled her L.A.M.B. multicolored turtleneck up over her head. She shook the static out of her silky hair, her long locks tumbling across her bare skin.

Julian's soft brown eyes widened as they ran across her

pale pink lace-trimmed Cosabella bra. 'I must be dreaming,' he said softly.

'It's real.' Tinsley stepped toward him and pressed her half-naked body against his. She kissed him fiercely. She had to have him – they had to do this, now. She had to stop thinking about how Julian had lost his virginity to Jenny Humphrey and start thinking about something else. Like losing her own.

'But . . .' Julian's voice trailed off as Tinsley's lips moved to his throat, kissing him right below his ear, which always drove him crazy. He groaned, and then, as if it was taking every ounce of willpower, pulled back away from Tinsley and stared into her eyes. 'What are you *doing*?' he asked, touching his hand gently to her hair.

'You.' She tugged his worn-out T-shirt over his head and the faint smell of Julian's deodorant permeated the room. A spark shot through her body and her hands tugged at the button on his faded dark Rock & Republic jeans. Tinsley felt like a conductor, all the parts of the orchestra moving at her command as she pushed him back down on his bed. It was crazy. She couldn't believe it was going to finally happen.

'Are you sure about this?' Julian asked, his eyes wide with surprise. 'I mean, really sure? Did Ryan Reynolds spray you with some of that tribal aphrodisiac shit?'

'You don't even need to ask.' She'd never been more sure of anything in her life.

They both kicked off the rest of their clothes and tumbled

together under Julian's comforter. She never imagined it would be so easy and laughed at herself for being all worked up about the various mechanics, and trying to plan the thing, down to the kind of music that would be playing in the background. How stupid. She didn't care what music was playing.

'Do you have . . . a condom?' she asked, trying not to feel shy. She'd always thought that people weren't ready to have sex if they couldn't say the word *condom* without embarrassment, but her face flushed anyway. Wasn't there a more elegant way to take care of things?

'Uh, yeah.' Julian sat up and pulled open his desk drawer, fumbling around and knocking a pencil to the floor. 'Here.' He pulled out a small plastic square, and Tinsley felt her heart sink. He kept condoms in his desk drawer. What for? She hadn't realized it until then, but she'd kind of hoped he wouldn't have any.

She tried to push the thought from her mind and get back into the mood as Julian's hands ran across her body again. But this time, the image of him touching Jenny the same way consumed Tinsley's brain. She wondered if Jenny had ever come bursting into his room, tearing off her clothes and ravaging him just as Tinsley had. The stupid grin she imagined on Jenny's pink-cheeked face as she and Julian did it made her groan out loud. 'Shit!'

Julian released the pressure on her back. 'You okay?' he asked worriedly.

Tinsley rolled off him and stood up. Now she was really

shaking, but she didn't want Julian to see. She grabbed her jeans from their crumpled heap on the floor and stepped into them. 'I'm sorry,' she said weakly. 'I can't do this.'

'It's okay,' Julian reassured her, wrapping his comforter around his body. 'We definitely don't need to rush.' He patted the bed and grinned up at her, his shaggy blondish hair tucked behind his ears. 'But please come back and let me kiss you.'

Tinsley sucked in her cheeks and turned her back on Julian in order to keep her composure. She snapped her bra back into place with shaking hands. How stupid of her to think she could make it all go away by sleeping with him. *That* wasn't what she wanted. What she wanted was for Jenny to have never existed – to have never shared something so special with the guy *she* was madly in love with. And unfortunately, she couldn't make that happen. 'I don't mean that . . . I mean, I can't see you anymore.'

'Wait, what?' Julian sat up in bed, suddenly wide awake. 'Why not?' His golden brown eyes widened, and Tinsley felt a twinge of regret at the sight of his bare chest peeking out from under his comforter.

'It's just not going to work,' she said coldly, tugging her sweater on. She forced herself to picture him tumbling naked in that very bed with Jenny Humphrey in order to keep her anger at the forefront of her emotions – and keep from crying. It worked. Tinsley had always been much better at being angry than sad. She grabbed her jacket from the floor.

'You can't be serious?' Julian jumped out of bed, quickly

throwing on his dark jeans. As much as Tinsley wanted him to stop her, she knew it wouldn't do any good. Jenny had won. She'd gotten to him first, and ruined him.

Tinsley grabbed the doorknob before Julian could touch her. She gave him the coldest stare she could muster. It was easier than she'd thought. 'I've never been more serious in my life,' she said, and slammed the door.

21

A SAVVY OWL KNOWS THAT ABSENCE MAKES THE HEART GROW FONDER.

Annoyance gripped Brandon as he took his latest Secret Satan gift out of the unmarked cardboard box left on his doorstep. This time, his brilliant Secret Satan had given him an alarm clock with a plastic pole dancer that slid up and down the pole. He set the alarm once, out of curiosity, and when it went off, a built-in strobe light lit up the tiny dollar bills painted on the miniature stage floor. It could've been one of those funny, tacky gifts that make great conversation starters. The only problem was the young chiseled plastic pole-dancer was a *guy*. One who looked disconcertingly like David Hasselhoff.

Brandon stuffed the whole thing back in the box, tossing it into the garbage can under his desk. Someone was definitely going to a lot of effort to torture him. At least no one had seen him open it. *Unlike* the box someone had put in his mailbox that morning, cleverly writing the address of Brandon's home in Greenwich in the return address spot. But instead of receiving some kind of end-of-semester care package from his father, he'd found himself in the middle of the mailroom, holding a plastic sperm-shaped piggy bank with a stupid smile on its face and a coin slot on its back. Ryan Reynolds had dropped in a quarter as he passed, and the fucking thing's tail wiggled. Brandon had dropped the whole thing in the recycling bin amid snorts and giggles from his classmates, wondering who was to blame.

He reached for his iPhone out of instinct, wishing he could just call Hellie and hear her voice. But the whole time-difference thing made her feel even farther away than she was. Brandon had just gotten back from practice, but she was probably fast asleep. That thought entertained him for a moment — he remembered her sliding into a loose gray T-shirt and a pair of black jersey short shorts before he'd left her room, and he always kept that image close to his heart. Instead, he logged onto his Yahoo! Instant Messenger and typed in **Sweet dreams**. He stared at the screen, willing her to be awake and write back, but nothing. He was just about to log off when her name popped up.

Hellie: Hey, sexy boy. I was just dreaming about you.
Brandon: I've been thinking about you all day. How was your drama rehearsal?

Brandon typed furiously, as if their connection could be lost at any moment. His heart raced at the thought of Hellie, sitting awake in the dark, tossing and turning in bed in her short shorts, dreaming about *him*.

Hellie: Sucked. You would think the crown prince of Egypt could muster up some passion as Macbeth, but he's like a wet fish.

Brandon laughed at Hellie's mixed metaphors. *A wet blanket? A cold fish?* Hellie's mother was Swiss and had met Mr Dunderdorf when he was on sabbatical in Geneva. Hellie and Gretchen had grown up in Switzerland, and when Dunderdorf came to teach at Waverly, they stayed behind at boarding school. God, what Brandon would have done to get her to transfer to Waverly.

Brandon: I think you mean cold fish.
Hellie: Oops, yes. Long day of classes and my brain isn't functioning well.
Brandon: I wish I could be there.
Hellie: Me too!

A smile curled Brandon's lips.

Brandon: You must have done something fun today?

He regretted this question immediately, worried that it would bring an avalanche of tales about guys trying to hit on her and her sister — because he knew better than anyone that every guy in the room would want to.

Hellie: Gretch and I snuck off to Geneva for a late dinner. We drank too much wine and complained about how much better American men are.

The smile on Brandon's face grew.

Brandon: I haven't had a drink since that kirsch your father gave us at Thanksgiving. It almost killed me.
Hellie: I'm glad it didn't. I brought home a bottle of my favorite wine that we can drink the next time we're together.

Brandon took a deep breath. He'd fantasized about jumping onto a plane and jetting off to Europe to see Hellie, but it wasn't exactly realistic. Finals, for one thing. But mostly, his hard-ass father would kill him if he charged a last-minute plane ticket to Europe to visit some girl he'd only hooked up with twice.

Brandon: Sounds good.

That was kind of lame, he thought. Couldn't he think of anything better?

Hellie: Want your hot body. Now.

Brandon blushed, his thumbs hovering over the keyboard, unsure of what to say. He'd loved the pictures Hellie had been texting – and he'd told her as much, in e-mails. But this was like . . . phone sex. What if Heath walked in? His heart raced and he was about to type **I think** about your smooth, naked skin every night when the screen popped again.

Hellie: My sister typed that. Bitch.

Brandon quickly typed LOL, grateful that he'd paused long enough to stave off humiliation.

Hellie: Ooh, our faculty monitor is doing rounds. Must run! Kisses!

Kisses, Brandon typed back, just before Hellie logged off.

He lay on his back on his bed, his hands behind his head. Outside darkness began to creep across Waverly. A darkness filled him, too. Hellie had lifted his spirits, but only momentarily. Brandon thought about how far away she was, and that she wasn't even coming home for Christmas. Dunderdorf had splurged to fly himself and his wife to Switzerland to see their girls and spend the holidays skiing in the Alps, much to Brandon's disappointment.

He hadn't thought he'd ever fall in love again after Callie had so brutally broken his heart last year, but this was different. He felt like if Hellie were just here – or he were there – everything in his whole life would fall into place. He wouldn't give a shit about his lazy, perverted roommate, or the gay rumors swirling around him. It wouldn't matter at all. Being with Hellie would make everything better.

At least then his Secret Santa would know he wasn't gay.

HeathFerro: Did your girlfriend like her presents?

JulianMcCafferty: What?

HeathFerro: Hope the extra virgin olive oil isn't extra virgin anymore . . .

JulianMcCafferty: Um, we're not actually together anymore.

JulianMcCafferty: But WTF are you talking about? I'm calling you right now.

OwlNet

From: SatansLittleHelper@hushmail.com
TO: Undisclosed recipients
Date: Saturday, December 14, 11:19 A.M.
Subject: Holiday Ball Alterna-party: Welcome to the Inferno

My little devils,

Excellent work with all the Secret Satan prezzies. I had no
idea how dirty you all were!

Now, let's Satanize the Holiday Ball. Marymount's determined
to make the official party boring. Screw that! Let's have our
own party. Let out all your sexual tension at the baddest, most
unofficial alterna-party imaginable – the Inferno.

Go to the back of the Faculty Club, and then follow the clues.
Everyone: get prepared to reveal yourselves to your Secret
Satans!

Formal attire still allowed – it'll be that much more fun to take
it off.

xxx,

S. L. H.

A GOOD OWL HAS A GOOD NOSE FOR A GOOD
PARTY.

In dire need of something to do, Brett anxiously adjusted a strand of sparkly silver tinsel on the twenty-foot Christmas tree that towered over the Prescott Faculty Club. She inhaled the rich pine scent of the needles as she followed the delicate garland around the tree, grateful for the chance to hide her face. The room looked amazing, like a glittering winter wonderland. She had spent the entire day in the elegant, dark mahogany ballroom, decorating with the activities committee. They had draped the room with about ten miles of white, twinkling lights, even fixing them to the ceiling so that it looked like a dark sky filled with stars. All the overhead lights were turned off, and the room was suffused with a soft glow. Dangling aqua and white starburst-shaped lanterns twinkled over the dance floor.

But no one was there.

Not 'no one,' technically, since all the activities committee volunteers were there. And all the alums who'd come in especially for the giant gala, crowded off to one side with the faculty. A dozen international students and assorted social outcasts lingered around the room, pointing at the green mistletoe bunches hanging over the archways or stepping nervously across the empty dance floor.

White-clothed round tables were loaded with trays of delicious-looking goodies – that Brett had painstakingly chosen and arranged – from Alistair's Green House, the gourmet all-organic caterer just outside of Rhinecliff. The food was completely untouched. A few of the volunteers hanging around the edges of the ballroom had snatched a portobello mushroom canapé or a bacon-wrapped scallop, but for the most part, the trays were as full as when the caterers delivered them. The crystal bowl of fruit punch was still filled nearly to the brim.

In a high-necked plum-colored silk charmeuse bubble dress by Laundry, her silver Stuart Weitzman pumps, and carrying the Stella McCartney clutch her sister had given her, Brett knew she looked fabulous, but her stomach was a knot of anxiety. She checked her dangling watch. It was after nine, and the party had officially started at eight. The only people actually dancing were Yvonne Stidder and her new boyfriend, Mukesh Patel, a scrawny senior whose father had been a major investor in Google before it took off. They were staring deeply into each other's eyes, the wide, empty dance floor stretching out around them like the smooth, untouched surface of a lake.

Brett gritted her teeth. Fashionably late was fine, but that didn't usually apply to the majority of underclassmen who had nothing better to do. Even total slackers like Heath Ferro and Alan St Girard could be counted on to show up soon after the doors opened in order to, as Heath liked to say, 'maximize his options'. What about tonight? It was a cold Saturday in December, and this was the biggest offi- cially sanctioned social event until the spring formal. Where the fuck *was* everyone?

Brett had spent the last half hour chatting up a couple of middle-aged alums, trying desperately to look interested as they waxed nostalgic about their Waverly days – before the insidious inventions of e-mail and cell phones. She adjusted a star-shaped Christmas tree light, took another deep breath of pine-scented air, and peeked at the main entrance to the ballroom. Maybe a rush of students was about to magically appear.

It didn't.

Brett glanced over her bare shoulder to see Dean Marymount and his surprisingly pretty blond wife chatting up some VIPs in suits. A gaggle of middle-aged women who clearly still wished they were in high school giggled and pointed at pictures in an old yearbook. Yearbooks had been casually planted on all the tables, one from each of the 128 years of Waverly's existence.

Was it possible that they all hadn't noticed that apart

from the international kids and the total losers, none of the student body was even at this stupid party? Brett steeled herself to go over to the eggnog punch bowl and chat some more with the I-bankers in Armani suits who used to call Waverly home. Her heart froze when an attractive woman in a simple black sheath dress and silver rope necklace poked her head out into the foyer, as if looking for all the missing students. It was Bethany Kephardt, the sophisticated assistant director of admissions at Brown. Brett had pored over the Class of '94 yearbook, memorizing Bethany's face and planning out exactly what to say to her.

But Brett didn't dare to approach her now. All her planning was worthless now that the party – *her* party – was gradually turning into a total flop. Brett's stomach fell and she felt the room start to spin, perhaps due to the mere thought of eggnog, which had always grossed her out. (Why would anyone want to drink eggs?) She'd felt isolated since her outburst in the dining hall, noticing how everyone would give her a wide berth on the walkways as she made her way to class and back to Dumbarton. But she hadn't thought everyone would hold it against her and blow off the party.

A rising anger toward Mr Wilde for dumping this stupid responsibility on her shoulders could only be subdued by chain-smoking Parliaments, which was all she wanted to do right now. The Disciplinary Committee had seemed like a good résumé booster, but it had brought her nothing but isolation. It was clear the students were off somewhere else, having the good time they were *supposed* to be having at the

Holiday Ball. The realization that everyone had successfully kept her out of the loop caused her to shake involuntarily. Did they all collectively decide to blow off the Holiday Ball? Jenny couldn't tell her? Or Kara? Had she so alienated everyone around her that she'd ostracized herself from her friends?

The faculty and alumni mumbled silently as Brett ladled herself a glass of fruit punch from the crystal bowl, needing to do something besides stand there with a stupid smile on her face. She glanced up and saw Mr Wilde, the DC adviser, and Mrs Horniman, her faculty adviser, leaning against the stage that lined the far end of the room. Dozens of strands of Christmas lights hung straight down from the ceiling to the edge of the stage, creating a beautiful, glowing curtain that Brett had intended to walk through when she welcomed everyone to this year's Holiday Ball.

They were talking, and then she saw them turn to look directly at her. The DJ in the corner, who had a confused look on his face and kept glancing around like he was doing a head count, dropped the needle on a jazzy version of 'Here Comes Santa Claus'. Brett felt her stomach heave. Bethany Kephardt approached Mr Wilde and touched him on the arm. She whispered something as he nodded his head in agreement, a slight grimace on his face.

Bethany Kephardt was unimpressed with Brett Messerschmidt. It was like the assistant director of admissions was Nero, flashing a violent thumbs-down to the gladiators.

Brett quickly spun around and walked to a different part

of the room, sidestepping the half-dozen couples who were scattered across the giant dance floor. Should she bring Bethany a glass of eggnog? Offer to explain why the party sucked so much?

She blinked her eyes rapidly and glanced up, only to notice how forlorn the tiny bunches of mistletoe she'd hung beneath all the doorways looked without cute couples kissing beneath them. She closed her eyes and tried hard to suppress thoughts of her humiliation, how it would stand for years and decades, the story of the Holiday Ball No One Attended being passed down from alum to alum, making the rounds as a rumor among all incoming freshmen for eternity. Brett would have to skip every alumni function at Waverly for fear of someone asking her about it.

She pressed her fingertips to her temples, wishing the floor would just open up and swallow her whole. The DJ segued into a remake of 'Jingle Bells'.

This was the lamest party. Ever.

A WISE OWL KNOWS THAT THE CAMERA SEES
EVERYTHING.

'Get the footprints in the snow,' Izzy hissed, and Kaitlin swung the camera across the marked snow. Jenny glanced around, shivering in the hunter green wellies she'd thrown on over her silky black nylons. They didn't exactly go with the red sleeveless belted minidress she'd borrowed from Kara Whalen – a sample from Kara's designer mom's spring line – but she wasn't about to stomp all over the snow-covered campus in heels.

'I don't know if I can,' Kaitlin said, lifting the camera from her face. She pursed her lips into a pout. 'There's not enough moonlight.'

The three freshmen had spent the last hour in Jenny's dorm room, filming her getting ready for the mysterious Inferno party. Jenny had tried her best to make it look interesting. She'd made sure to toss the outfits she decided against onto her bed carelessly, as Callie or Tinsley might have done, but her knockoffs just looked sloppy piled up on her bed, instead of elegant or Marie Antoinette decadent. Claire wanted to film her putting on her makeup, but Jenny got so flustered with the camera in her face that she'd bumped her mascara wand against her nose, leaving an enormous coal-black splotch. She'd had to wash her face and start all over again.

The four of them had followed the trail of people in the direction of the Prescott Faculty Club, where a few of the nerdier students had headed up the steps into the official Holiday Ball. Had they not been invited to the Inferno? Jenny wondered. She felt a stab of guilt about blowing off the official holiday party; after all, Brett had spent the last two weeks planning it. Jenny had felt guilty when she got the e-mail from Satan's Little Helper that morning inviting her to the alterna-party. But the Inferno was clearly going to be the cool party, and Jenny felt obligated to go for her film crew. Besides, there were definitely *some* people going to the Holiday Ball, so maybe Brett wouldn't even notice her absence?

The rest of the people, however, turned and headed down the path that led behind the building. 'How do they know where to go?' Claire whispered, glancing around them. There was nothing but footprints leading down the walkway, into the darkness. Excited whispers echoed through the sharp night air.

'There!' Jenny said, giggling and pointing a pink-mittened hand down the pathway. Poking out of the snow at the corner of the path was a stick – with an unrolled yellow condom on top of it. On the top of the condom, a tiny Santa's hat was perched. 'And there's another one up ahead.'

'Good eye, Jenny,' Izzy exclaimed, wiping her nose again with a tissue. Her cold was back, and Jenny had been trying to keep her distance. They followed the winding path, the Santa-hatted condoms leading the way past several of the science buildings and toward the southern edge of campus, near the sports fields.

'We'd better not be going to the soccer field, because I think I already have frostbite.' Claire wobbled on her too-high black heels. 'Jenny, it was sooo smart of you to wear boots.' Ever since the Raves had agreed to come play the party, the girls were back to fawning all over Jenny. They'd even thought it was cute when she'd mascaraed her nose.

'Think your Secret Satan's going to give you another romantic present, Jenny?' Kaitlin prompted, still holding the camera on Jenny. 'Like maybe a kiss?'

'I saw Cliff Montgomery, that water polo guy, staring at you yesterday when you were making your salad at dinner. Like, really staring.' Claire rubbed her cheeks for warmth. 'You guys would look totally hot together.'

Jenny exhaled, her breath a cloud in the dark December air. Her Secret Satan had left a copy of J. D. Salinger's *Franny and Zooey* in her mailbox that morning, and she'd spent the afternoon reading it, searching for clues about why he'd given it to her. She still couldn't figure it out, but she loved the book – and she was dying to tell him so. If it was a him. But it had to be, right? A girl would have given her lip gloss or something. For a second, she let herself imagine Cliff Montgomery, who had a mop of dark, curly brown hair that made him look like a young, cute Bob Dylan, waiting for her outside class to walk her home.

'I'm betting on Ryan Reynolds.' Izzy pulled her thick scarf tighter around her neck. 'I know he's kind of skeevy, but I hear he's got a soft side.'

'And I think his family owns a vineyard in Napa. And a jet.' Kaitlin stepped gingerly over a patch of ice, the camera wobbling in her hand. 'He could whisk you away for romantic weekends in wine country.'

'You're so lucky, Jenny,' Claire said mournfully. 'I really am not excited to meet the person who got me a bottle of Astroglide.'

'Look.' Jenny pointed ahead to the Cambridge House, a little colonial-style redbrick house on the very southern edge of campus, barely visible through a thicket of overgrown pine trees. Her stomach was fluttering madly at the thought of who could be behind her sweet Secret Santa presents. 'I think that's where we're going.'

As they approached the building, red light seemed to be spilling from the shade-covered windows. She'd never actually been inside Cambridge House – it was reserved for the writer-in-residence, whose sole responsibilities were to teach one writing workshop a year and oversee the publication of *Absinthe*. It was a cushy gig. This year's writer-in-residence, Josip Rosnichov, a hard-drinking, fifty-something Russian, had given his final reading at the Reynolds Atrium last week and had gone back to Saint Petersburg. Cambridge House was wide open until the next unstable and probably bizarre writer arrived in January. It was the perfect spot for an unofficial party.

'What about the ball at the Prescott Club?' Claire asked, pausing to shake snow off her feet before they stepped inside. 'Are we going to that later?' A note of concern crept into her voice.

Jenny turned her head so the camera could catch her in profile. At Yvonne Stidder's Thanksgiving party in New York, Tinsley hammered it into Jenny's brain that she should be enjoying life and not taking boys too seriously. Jenny imagined herself flitting around the party, flirting like mad, making her Secret Santa and all the other guys fall madly in love with her. She'd be sure to piss off Tinsley, who'd been so cold to her recently, for good measure. Finally she answered: 'Would you rather go to a school-sponsored party, or the best illegal party on campus, with the Raves?'

She didn't wait for a response and knocked on the black heavy wooden door of Cambridge House. It instantly swung open, revealing Heath Ferro in a Santa hat, a tight white T-shirt, and a pair of green suspenders holding up a pair of red furry pants trimmed in white. A pair of bells swung on a gold-braided rope around his neck.

'Welcome to the Inferno,' he said grandly. 'Touch my bells.'

'Gross.' Jenny edged past him into the smoke-filled foyer. A narrow staircase led up to the second floor, already crowded with girls in party dresses.

'Or my pants. What about you lovely ladies?' Heath asked as the freshmen skirted past him, giggling.

'He's so hot,' Claire whispered, glancing back at him over her shoulder. 'Maybe he's your Secret Santa.'

'I think my gifts would have definitely been X-rated. I'm pretty sure he's the one who started the whole Secret Satan thing.' Jenny surveyed the scene. The front room of Cambridge House had been completely wrapped in red cellophane, and fake yellow construction-paper flames ran up the walls. A giant white dry-erase board was propped up over the fireplace, featuring a drawing of stick figures with angel wings engaged in devilish behavior. All the lightbulbs had been replaced with red bulbs and Jenny recognized fellow Owls, dressed in cocktail party attire, smushed into couches and gossiping in the corners.

'Ohmigod.' Izzy's eyes were wide with amazement. 'Kaitlin, make sure you're getting all this.'

After shoving their coats into an overstuffed hall closet, Jenny spotted Benny Cunningham with Sage and Alison under an arrow that read HELL'S KITCHEN. As she picked her way through the crowd, she paused here and there to allow Claire and Izzy and Kaitlin to catch up. Kaitlin kept stopping to film someone in a great outfit, or a couple kissing under a chili-pepper mistletoe. Jenny wrinkled her nose. The couple pulled apart. It was Ryan Reynolds and Alison Quentin. Guess he wasn't her Secret Satan.

She turned around and almost walked directly into a vaguely familiar-looking guy with reddish brown hair and square black glasses. 'Excuse me,' she said. She smoothed her hands down the sides of her dress.

The guy coughed into his hand and nervously picked at the fading Spider-Man logo on the front of the T-shirt he wore under a dark blazer. Jenny remembered where she'd seen him – always heading into the computer science lab when she was going to art class. He was one of those comp-sci nerds. 'I'm, uh . . . glad you liked your barrettes.'

'Wait, what?' Jenny started, not sure she'd heard him right. She touched the dragonfly barrettes she'd put in her hair.

'They look pretty.' The skinny guy shoved his hands in his pockets nervously. 'Did you get a chance to read *Franny and Zooey*? It's like my favorite Salinger book. Better than *Catcher in the Rye*.'

Jenny's stomach fell. *This* was the guy who'd been sending her the sweet, romantic presents? Not the sexy upperclassman she'd been dreaming about. This dorky, nearsighted guy with uneven sideburns and a too-big nose who was barely taller than she was. Why was this always *happening*? Why was she always getting her hopes up – only to get them crushed to pieces? This didn't happen to Tinsley, or Brett, or Callie. Just her. In a flash, she remembered how

Easy had dumped her to go back to Callie. How Julian had hooked up with Tinsley. How Drew Gately had tried to lie his way into her bed. Her heart thumped so loudly in her chest, she was sure everyone could hear it.

A cold chill ran down the back of her neck as Kaitlin focused her camera on Jenny. *Not now*, she thought, remembering all their giggling discussions about which hot upper-class guy could be giving Jenny such sweet gifts. That would make a great scene – juxtaposing that against *this*. The Spider-Man-wearing comp-sci guy stood in front of her expectantly.

'Um, yeah.' She rubbed her hands up and down her bare shoulders. 'Thanks.' She gave the guy a half-smile, and even though she knew she was being rude, all she wanted was to get away from the camera before Kaitlin could get any more footage. Didn't they know anything? Didn't they realize how embarrassing this was for her?

Verena Arneval waved at Jenny from the kitchen doorway, holding up a glass of red liquid. 'Jenny!' she cried out, already tipsy. 'Get over here. When are the Raves coming?'

'I'm Michael,' the nerd said, glancing in confusion at the three freshmen girls who were crowded around Jenny – and staring at him with disappointed looks on their faces. Loud music with a pulsing beat pounded through the room, making Jenny's heart beat faster. Michael held out his hand as Kaitlin trained the camera on his Spider-Man T-shirt.

Before she could do anything, Jenny felt a vibration at her hip and reached into her tiny silk bag for her phone.

The number flashed as private, but Jenny was grateful for any sort of distraction. 'Hello?' She felt the camera swing to her.

'It's Damian,' a voice said, sounding far away.

Jenny winked at the camera. 'It's the Raves,' she announced loudly, feeling confident again as a titter went around the small circle. Alison and Benny and some others had stepped forward to listen. 'What's up?' Jenny asked into the phone. 'You lost?'

'Sorry, babe,' Damian said, 'we can't make it. We won't get up there in time.' A female voice on the other end of the phone shrieked in the background. 'Shush!' Damian whispered.

'Oh.' Jenny tried to turn away, but people suddenly seemed to be surrounding her in every direction. She kept a plastic smile plastered to her face even though she felt like she'd been hit by a car. This couldn't be happening. 'Well, the party will go pretty late. Where exactly are you?'

Another shriek and another shush. 'We got sort of . . . sucked into this other thing after our show, so we'll be here for a while longer. Really sorry.'

Jenny hoped the camera couldn't detect the lump in her throat. She heard a click in her ear and said, 'Hello? Are you there?' No response. A line of sweat formed on her forehead, but she didn't wipe it. 'Well, don't worry about it, Dam. We totally understand,' she said into the phone, even though he'd hung up.

'What did they say?' Claire asked excitedly, twirling her long pearl necklace around her forefinger.

'Are they on their way?' Izzy demanded, reflexively touching her hair.

'They . . . can't make it,' Jenny sputtered out. Everyone around her groaned. This was worse than being humiliated by a boy.

'That's a shame.' Benny exchanged a look with Sage before they linked arms and disappeared. Almost instantly, the looks on her three followers' faces turned from disappointment . . . to disbelief. As if she'd made it all up. As if she *weren't* friends with Damien Polk!

Well, okay, so she wasn't, really. But she *knew* him. And the Raves were her one claim to fame – the one truly exciting thing that had happened to Jenny in her boring fifteen years of life. And now . . . everyone probably thought she was a poser.

'Are you sure that was him?' Claire asked, tilting her head.

Kaitlin kept the camera rolling, zooming in for a close-up on Jenny. 'Maybe you heard him wrong?'

'How well do you know him, again?' Izzy asked timidly.

All the anxiety of the past few days rushed volcanically through Jenny's veins – she felt a trickle of sweat run from under her arms down and around her back and her face suddenly felt as red as her surroundings. 'Oh my God will you please get out of my face for one second?!' she cried, pressing her hands to her temples.

Michael, who had been hovering nearby the whole time, slunk away, looking sad and confused. Kaitlin dropped the camera, and Jenny wiped the sweat away before it could ruin her makeup. She knew people were watching her, but she couldn't help it – how could Kaitlin be so stupid to keep the camera rolling through humiliation after humiliation? 'Do you always have to be on top of me?'

Shaking, and feeling as if she was going to pass out, Jenny pushed past Claire and Izzy and Kaitlin, who stepped away as if they'd been slapped. A path opened for her, as if no one wanted her to touch them. Tears of frustration filled Jenny's eyes, but she'd be damned if she'd let everyone see her cry.

If this was what it felt like to be a star, Jenny preferred to be a nobody.

24

A WAVERLY OWL KNOWS HOW TO USE MISTLETOE.

Bethany Kephardt wrapped herself in her long black wool Michael Kors coat, slipping her hands into a pair of leather gloves. Brett stood off to the side and watched helplessly. The Holiday Ball was so boring that even alumni were already starting to trickle out the doors. The DJ had gone on a smoke break and failed to return – he'd probably ended up wherever everyone else was – and had just left the CD of Muppets Christmas songs on repeat. If she had to hear Miss Piggy scream *'Five gold rings'* one more time, she'd hurl the plate of uneaten bite-size salmon crostini into the Christmas tree. An ancient-looking couple jitterbugged on the dance floor, oblivious to the fact that 'The Twelve Days of Christmas' wasn't exactly a great dancing song.

Only sparsely filled, the winter wonderland Brett had worked so hard to create looked more like an unused set of a holiday television special. The yearbooks had been flipped through and politely closed on the tables, the catered food left mostly untouched by the alumni and faculty and assorted freshmen and sophomores scattered around. A strand of lights on the tree went dark, and Brett turned her back on the whole scene, shaking with disappointment and anger.

The doors to the Prescott Faculty Club blew shut and Brett knew Bethany Kephardt was gone for good, taking Brett's chances of getting into Brown with her. A moment later, another rush of cold air came from the door, and Brett whirled around to see who else was leaving.

Instead, Sebastian was making his way through the crowd around the door. His dark head bobbed above the thin crowd as the guests eyed him, wondering if he was the first in a stream of students that were simply running really late. Heads turned and necks swiveled, but it was clear that Sebastian didn't have any other students in tow.

He smiled when he saw Brett, and she'd never been more grateful to see him – although she was still annoyed. Why hadn't he come *on time*? His wet shoes squeaked as he crossed the dance floor. 'I thought I'd find you here.' He pushed his dark, gel-free hair out of his face and eyed her dress appreciatively.

'Why?' She fingered her hair nervously. She'd swept the sides up into two large clips, and it felt a little strange not having the comforting swish of her hair against her face. 'Because I gave up my life for two weeks to plan this whole thing? And then nobody comes?' She felt her voice rising and struggled to keep it under control. At least there was no one around to hear it.

'What do you have to eat here?' Sebastian asked, the corners of his eyes reddish, as if he'd just been smoking pot. She could tell he was purposely ignoring her little whining fit, which just made her angrier.

Brett waved her bare arm out in front of her, indicating the tables and tables of barely touched canapés and vegetable dips. 'Anything you could possibly want.' She crossed her arms in front of her chest, thinking of all the hours she'd spent tasting stupid hors d'oeuvres when she could have just poured a bag of Doritos into a bowl and called it a night.

The corners of Sebastian's lips twitched, and he tugged at the collar of his crisp white shirt. 'Who are all the losers?'

'Keep your voice down,' she admonished him, though she didn't really care if the alumni overheard or not. Then she noticed a red stain on his white shirt. It looked like a lipstick smudge. 'Where'd you get this?' she asked as she pointed to the mark. And then, though she'd been trying to block it out, the image of him escorting Callie down the steps of Dumbarton flashed back to her.

Sebastian looked down, surprised. 'At the Inferno party,' he answered matter-of-factly. 'Punch stain.'

'Great.' Brett straightened up. 'So you and all the other cool people went to some other cool party while I'm stuck here, talking to Mrs Horniman and . . . the guy who keeps telling me Vietnam stories.' Even though she'd suspected that everyone had been keeping the real party a secret from her, it hurt to know it was true. She turned her back on Sebastian, seething, and stomped over to the food tables. She grabbed a strawberry, dipped it in chocolate, and popped it into her mouth.

'Look, I'm sorry.' Sebastian appeared at her side, and she stared at him incredulously. Had he just apologized to her? That was a first. She pressed her lips together and tried to listen as he explained how someone – most likely Heath – had planned a whole alterna-party at Cambridge House, thinking that the official Holiday Ball was going to be tightly policed and boring. 'But I didn't want to leave you here all alone,' he added, glancing around the room.

Brett felt her disappointment and anger start to melt away. The Holiday Ball *was* really lame. If she hadn't planned it, she wouldn't have come, either. 'Gee, thanks.'

'No really,' Sebastian insisted. 'I thought of you all alone, probably listening to Marymount's jokes, and I knew it wasn't right . . .' He trailed off, an uncharacteristically shy look coming over his face.

Brett traced her plum-colored fingernails along the white tablecloth. 'What about Callie?' she asked softly. 'Did you take her to the other party?' It felt weird to mention Callie's name out loud.

Sebastian coughed into his fist, then rubbed his chin nervously. 'Look, about Callie.' Brett's stomach fell – he was going to tell her that he was in love with Callie, and that he was just being nice to Brett right now because she was Callie's friend.

'I was only dating Callie to piss you off,' he said sheepishly, after a minute of torturous silence. 'I mean, she's nice and everything . . .'

Brett considered this. Taking Callie out to dinner, giving her tacky – but sweet – little presents, sitting next to her in the dining hall, letting her change his cologne. He did all that to piss Brett off? 'You did that just to win our stupid bet?' she asked, playing with the Alexis Bittar Lucite bangles on her wrist. She stared right at him, her almond-shaped green eyes searching his face for a clue. 'Grandma Got Run Over by a Reindeer' was now playing on the speakers. At least the DJ had turned off the Muppets.

'For someone so smart, you really can be dumb,' Sebastian scoffed, touching the stain on his shirt again.

'What does that mean?' Brett snapped. Why couldn't he ever just say what he meant?

Or, for that matter, why couldn't *she*?

He stepped closer to her, and Brett felt her heart skip a couple beats. She felt the way she did in field hockey, the moment she noticed that she had a clear shot at the goal. 'You know what that means,' he murmured, his voice low.

His dark brown eyes scanned Brett's face with a longing look that had been there all along — she'd just been too dumb to see it.

She opened her mouth to say something, but before she could, Sebastian's lips found hers. She closed her eyes, enjoying the feel of his warm, strong mouth, the slight pot and alcohol taste of his breath giving her a buzz that traveled the length of her body.

'Are you mad at me?' Sebastian asked as he pulled away, his finger tracing her cheek. She'd never seen his eyes from so close before, and she noticed that his dark brown irises were rimmed in black.

'Now who's the dumb one,' Brett murmured, feeling slightly dizzy. But it was better than she'd felt in a long, long time, and before she could stop herself, she grabbed Sebastian by his tie and pulled him in for another kiss.

Callie Vernon stomped up the steps into the Prescott Faculty Club, annoyed that she had to chase Sebastian down — he really needed to learn how to be a more accessible boyfriend. She was freezing in her thin Michael Kors knit coat. Didn't he know that going out meant you attended major social events together? No one at the Inferno party had seen him in over an hour, and she'd already tried his room, interrupting his roommate, Drew, and some half-clothed girl who'd hid under the covers when Callie barged in. She suspected the Holiday Ball was

the last place she'd find Sebastian, but she was desperate
– what good was having a boyfriend if people didn't see
you together and get jealous?

The first thing she noticed when she entered the ballroom was how empty it was. The decorations were elaborate:
a towering Christmas tree nearly as beautiful as the blue
spruce they'd had in the Governor's Mansion ballroom last
Christmas, though not as lavishly decorated, dazzled the
room with light. A row of white-clothed tables lined the
far wall, and Callie could see from where she stood that
most of the platters of food were still intact. Where was
everyone? The Inferno party was packed, but she hadn't realized that practically everyone at school was there. Callie had
assumed that enough of the less-cooler kids would make it
to the ball that no one – except for maybe Brett – would
notice the others' absence.

Apparently that wasn't the case. She nodded politely
at Mr Gaston, her excruciatingly boring Latin teacher,
wondering if she should go over and suck up to him. But
she had more pressing concerns. She'd spent two hours in
Tinsley's room with her special curling iron bought at
Ken Paves's Beverly Hills, and her wide, tumbling curls
of strawberry blond hair were starting to lose their spring.
In her pale pink Carolina Herrera dress with a flouncy
skirt and narrow black belt, she accepted many admiring
stares from the dorky freshmen gathered near the punch
bowl.

Where was Sebastian? Callie wrapped a curl around her

finger, trying to revitalize it, as she scanned the room, looking for his tall figure. By missing the Inferno party, they were wasting a perfectly good opportunity for Sebastian to make some new friends – Callie's friends. Benny and Sage and most of the other girls were already fawning over him, so they needed to establish themselves as a couple. Pretty soon, everyone would be completely envious of them, just like they had been of her and Easy.

Callie spun around toward the exit, ready to give up and head back to the Inferno. Maybe Sebastian had just taken a pot-smoking break. Then she caught the image of a couple standing in the middle of one of the arched door-ways that led out to the hallway, kissing. She focused her eyes, half-expecting to see two teachers acting inappropri-ately, before she recognized the flame-red hair, twisted back at the sides. Sneaky Brett, having some kind of secret, steamy love affair.

But then the couple separated, and Callie realized she knew the guy. It was Sebastian.

'Oh my God!' she squealed loudly enough for everyone in a fifty-foot radius to hear. But Callie didn't care. This was her pseudo-boyfriend . . . making out with one of her pseudo-best friends. 'How *could* you?' Callie shouted, not sure if she was talking to Brett or Sebastian.

Brett and Sebastian sprang apart, their eyes wide with surprise and guilt. Callie could feel the blood coursing through her veins, and she whirled around and staggered toward the exit, feeling as if she'd just been slapped. Not even two months ago, at the Monster Mash Bash, Easy had called her a spoiled little bitch in this very ballroom.

And now, she'd been dumped by a guy she'd only just started seeing.

So much for the holiday spirit.

25

A WAVERLY OWL IS ALWAYS PREPARED FOR THE WORST.

After the disaster with the Raves no-show, Jenny had furiously gulped down some spiked eggnog and managed to make her way into the empty unheated den at the back of the house. The cold air was a relief after the sweaty party, and Jenny pressed her forehead against the cool glass sliding door that looked out on a snow-covered brick patio. Outside, the shapes of various lawn furniture and a charcoal grill looked faintly poetic in the snow, and she fought the urge to text her brother, Dan, who was right now probably curled up with his laptop in his dorm room at Evergreen, far away in Oregon, writing an angst-ridden poem.

With a sigh, Jenny cautiously sipped her cup of Hell Fire, the red punch Heath had spiked with every alcohol in the known universe. She was relieved to be free of Claire and Izzy and Kaitlin — and everyone else. It felt good to be alone for once. She hadn't realized what a mistake it was to let her freshman fan club film her. It might have made her feel special for a while, but soon she just felt ridiculous, analyzing every little inch of her life. She was self-conscious enough as it was — what the hell had she been thinking?

But it was still wrong to snap at the girls like that, not to mention the poor Michael kid. Now that she'd calmed down, she definitely owed them all an apology. She'd make it up to them in the morning by buying them croissants at Maxwell, and then maybe she'd ask them to abandon the whole film project altogether. Actually, she should do it now.

Jenny pushed open the creaky den door and stepped through the laundry room. Trisha Reikken was sitting on the washing machine, legs wrapped around some senior guy. An old Killers song blasted from the iPod stereo somewhere in the distance, and Jenny already felt calmer. So what if the Raves had blown her off. No one seemed to care. Jenny tipped her cup again, the last of the sickly sweet concoction coating the back of her throat as the alcohol warmed her whole body. No one was paying attention to her, and it felt refreshing. She hadn't felt this relaxed in what seemed like forever. She wanted to keep it going, but first . . . she had to use the bathroom.

A girl named Satoko from her art class was sitting at the kitchen table, a Santa hat perched on her head, fumbling with her BlackBerry. 'Do you know where the bathroom is?' Jenny asked.

Satoko pointed toward a long line of girls snaking up the stairs. She bit her lip. 'Are you going to, uh, brush your teeth?'

'Huh?' Jenny stared at her, wondering if Satoko had been sharing the Venus de Milo–shaped bong that had been one of Alan St Girard's Secret Satan presents. She wandered into the next room, pushing her way through the crowd of girls in formal dresses toward the bathroom line. A burst of raucous laughter from the living room caught Jenny's attention, and as she looked up, she saw a cluster of people staring at an iPhone. Alan St Girard looked up and caught Jenny's eye, grinning goofily at her and raising his Hell Fire glass in salute.

She smiled and gave him a wave back. Weird. Maybe the fame business had its perks, after all. Her gold skimmers stepped carefully over a red stain in the rug – she pitied the next Waverly writer-in-residence – and stood in line behind Sage Francis, who was also watching something on her phone.

'Is there only one bathroom in here or something?' Jenny asked, wondering why Sage had to wear so much sparkly eye shadow.

Sage pressed her phone to her chest – most of which was visible in a red flouncy Free People dress with a deep

V-neck – and shifted away from Jenny. 'Oh, yeah. I think so.' Sage pushed a strand of stringy blond hair out of her eyes and gave Jenny a funny look. Jenny could feel heads turn in her direction. Suddenly, she wished that she didn't have to wait in line for the bathroom, the way famous people never had to wait in line for anything.

A girl ahead in line pointed at Jenny, and another girl Jenny vaguely recognized started giggling. Jenny just smiled back. The front room was suddenly lit with tiny spotlights as people pulled out their phones, their screens lighting up with whatever the latest attraction was.

'Where is she?' someone cried out, and the sound of bells jingling meant it could only be Heath Ferro. A moment later, he tumbled through the doorway and drunkenly stumbled into the bathroom line. A huge grin crossed his handsome face when he spotted Jenny. He threw his arms around her, enveloping her in his dirty-ashtray scent. His blondish-brown hair was completely disheveled, as if someone had just given him a noogie.

'What?' Jenny demanded angrily, pushing Heath off her and crossing her bare arms over her chest. She felt the tiny hairs on the back of her neck stand up. What was going on?

'I'd like to see this outfit.' Heath flashed his iPhone up to Jenny's face, and it took her a moment to realize she was staring at a slow-motion video of herself. In it, Jenny was saying something into the camera, but the sound was off. Her navy J.Crew shirt was misbuttoned to reveal a burst of red bra. Ohmigod. Jenny remembered that day, waxing poetic about her art class as the freshmen interviewed her about some of her favorite classes. But Jenny's voice was silent as her lips moved on the screen, the Radiohead song 'Creep' playing over the image as it cut to Jenny in the dining hall, talking with broccoli in her teeth, again in slow motion. The song looped around and began again as an image of Jenny slipping and falling on some black ice in front of Dumbarton segued into Jenny waking that first morning to find the camera poked in her face, a glob of drool sliding down her cheek.

'Give me that!' Jenny screamed, grabbing for Heath's iPhone. He snatched it back, out of her reach, but it didn't matter. Kaitlin and Claire and Izzy had clearly rushed from the party after Jenny's outburst and quickly edited together the most embarrassing moments of Jenny-film. It wouldn't have been too hard to find them. Now the whole party was watching the same video, over and over, the room suddenly full of smiling faces and loud cackling.

Jenny bolted out of line, heading for the kitchen, or the back den – anywhere to be out of the glare of those staring eyes. Callie and Tinsley would never let themselves be filmed with food in their teeth, or with drool on their chin. The sickening thought that she would never be able to escape her loserdom made her gasp for air in the crowded kitchen. She didn't see any friendly faces, only averted glances and half-smiles as everyone cleared the way.

Like her lameness was somehow contagious.

OwlNet Instant Message Inbox

CelineColista: OMG. Did you see the Jenny video?

VerenaArneval: Didn't watch the whole thing yet – poor J!

CelineColista: Remind me never to let anyone make a film about me . . .

VerenaArneval: Um . . . don't think you have to worry about that!

26

A WAVERLY OWL KNOWS THAT WHAT HAPPENS IN JUNIOR HIGH STAYS IN JUNIOR HIGH.

B ack at the Inferno, Callie miserably held two empty plastic cups while some random freshman she'd never seen before filled them with red punch, chattering on about his car, or his friend's car – she couldn't be sure. She muttered her thanks and sauntered into the living room, drinking from both cups and not caring if anything spilled down the satin bodice of her expensive dress. She elbowed her way over to the iPod stereo on one of the white built-in bookcases and fought the urge to scroll through the playlist for some Alanis or Avril or some other angry chick rocker. She couldn't believe her rebound boyfriend had *cheated* on her – and with *Brett* no less. Didn't Sebastian know his job was to make her feel *better* about herself, not *worse*?

She ran her fingers through her limp strawberry blond

curls and pretended to read the book titles on the shelves. A cheap paperback copy of *Wuthering Heights* reminded her of the first time she'd hooked up with Easy, in the rare books room at the library. She'd seen him running his fingers across a rare first edition of the book and then minutes later, he was running those same fingers lovingly across her collarbone. It gave her a chill just thinking about it.

She had virtually no more guy options at Waverly. Maybe she would have to start dating townies. Or the wannabes from St Lucius who weren't cool enough to attend parties on their own campus. Brett – and Tinsley – had already tried teachers, and *that* hadn't worked out. She furiously drank a full cup of Hell Fire and set it down on the mantel, next to a framed photograph of a gravestone. Weird. She squinted at it, and saw that it was F. Scott Fitzgerald's grave. Still weird.

'In it to win it, eh?' Tinsley appeared suddenly at Callie's side, blowing smoke up over their heads. A Virginia Slim hung lazily from one hand. She looked annoyingly stunning in a slim-fitting yellow dress that would have made anyone but her look like a lemon.

'Something like that.' Callie scrunched her hands in her hair to bring the curls back to life, but to no avail. She noticed that Tinsley kept twisting the silver Celtic band she wore on her right ring finger nervously. 'Still avoiding Julian?'

Tinsley's blue-violet eyes narrowed slightly as she continued to casually assess the party – and not answer.

She blew a puff of smoke into the air. 'It'll take an army of underpaid cleaning ladies to put this place back together. Someone punched a hole in the bathroom upstairs. And the toilet seat is missing.'

'Thanks for the heads-up.' Callie plucked a copy of *Alice in Wonderland* from the shelf and flipped through the pages, wondering why a childless middle-aged writer would have it on his shelves. Maybe he had a weird obsession with young blond girls. Maybe Callie could date *him*.

'So.' Tinsley grabbed the book from Callie's hands, scattering ashes from her cigarette across the leather, and popped it back into place on the shelf. 'Did you like my gifts?'

'What?' Callie asked, leaning in to hear as the music shook the room. *Gifts?*

'You know. My Secret Satan presents.' Tinsley had a self-satisfied grin on her red lips. 'Did you like them?' Tinsley squinted as she took a long drag from her cigarette, burning it down close to the filter. She exhaled a torrent of smoke, making Callie's eyes water.

Callie's pale pink mouth dropped open in astonishment. 'I can't believe that was you!' Tinsley – her supposed best friend – had been laughing at her this whole time. Brett, meanwhile, her other supposed best friend, was busy stealing away Sebastian. 'Old Maid cards? A knitting kit? You're a fucking bitch!'

Tinsley giggled, her elegant shoulders rising and falling with her laughter. A tallish sophomore in a rumpled black suit and loosened candy cane tie bumped into Callie, pushing her forward.

'Do you have any idea what you put me through?' Callie grabbed Tinsley's bare arm to steady herself, but she really wanted to grab Tinsley by her shoulders and shake her. Tinsley had been the one torturing her all this time? *Why would you do that?*

'So that you could see how ridiculous you're being.' Tinsley rolled her eyes. 'You're sixteen, in case you forgot.'

Callie bit her lip. Okay, just because she was still kind of young didn't mean anything. 'Whatever. Lots of people have met their future spouses by the time they're sixteen.'

Tinsley sighed heavily and stubbed out her cigarette in a cheap aluminum ashtray. 'Yeah? Give me an example. Besides your parents and like, people in Nebraska.' She grabbed Callie's arm and spun her around so she could see the whole crowded party. 'Why would you *want* to meet your husband when you're sixteen? You're one of the hottest chicks at this party . . . and this school. And, like, the world,' Tinsley lectured loudly in her ear.

Callie sniffed. But . . . Tinsley had a point. 'Okaaay.'

'So get over yourself, will you?' Tinsley smiled, her perfect white teeth gleaming. 'Or you really will turn into an old maid.'

Callie rubbed a hand against her forehead. She spotted Ryan Reynolds leering at her from the dance floor. When he caught her eye, he made a gesture for her to come over, which she ignored. Then she saw a couple of freshman guys in the corner, who awkwardly turned away when she caught them looking at her. A sly, knowing grin crept over her face.

Maybe the idea of dying an old maid *was* ridiculous. Tinsley was right. Sebastian didn't know what he was missing. And why would Callie want to be saddled with a guy who drove a Mustang anyway? She tossed her head, letting her wavy strawberry blond hair tumble across her shoulders. 'Let's have fun being single together. Girl power and all that, right?' She nudged Tinsley in the waist. No matter how hot Tinsley was, it did make her feel better that she was single too.

Tinsley blanched at the word *single*. She'd been so thrilled to see Callie laugh again after her neediness these past few weeks . . . but did she have to rub Tinsley's nose in the fact that she was single too? As if she could forget.

'Speak of the devil,' Callie said in a low voice, staring at someone over Tinsley's shoulder. Tinsley felt her whole body tense up. She'd only seen Julian once, in the crowded dining hall, since she'd broken things off with him, although he'd texted her several times. But she didn't want to give him a chance to explain. She just needed to get over him first, before he had a chance to work his way back in.

Julian appeared next to her, wearing a faded gray American Apparel V-neck and a pair of black jeans. 'Hey,' he said, pushing a lock of his light brown hair behind his ear. He glanced around nervously, sidestepping Emily

Jenkins. She wore a short red velvet skirt trimmed with white fur, like a dirty Mrs Claus. 'Can we talk?'

Callie shot Tinsley a 'don't do anything I wouldn't do' look before flipping her hair over her shoulder one more time and sashaying away. 'I'll be on the dance floor.'

Tinsley watched her friend shoulder her way through the crowded room, taking in all the cute boys checking her out as she passed. Callie was going to be fine. She finally let her eyes fall on Julian's face, and she forced herself to picture him losing his virginity to Jenny Humphrey in order to not melt at the sight of his familiar brown eyes. She shrugged with a coolness she didn't feel. 'Talk.'

'Not here.' Julian touched Tinsley's back. She jumped away from him as if she'd been burned. 'Sorry, just . . . come this way.'

He led her through the kitchen to a tiny laundry room and pulled closed a vinyl accordion door. The room smelled like fabric softener, an improvement from the other room's alcohol and sweat smell.

Julian exhaled loudly as Tinsley leaned against the washing machine, arms crossed bitchily in front of her, eyebrows raised expectantly. 'Listen,' he said, looking nervous. 'You need to know something.'

Tinsley felt her stomach drop. If she actually heard him say the words *I slept with Jenny Humphrey*, she'd probably throw up, right there. 'If it's about you and your *lover*, I don't care.' She turned to leave.

Julian reached out and grabbed Tinsley's bare arm. 'How

about you *listen* to me for once?' The force in Julian's normally calm voice made Tinsley stop in her tracks. She wasn't used to people talking to her like that. His dark eyes glittered in the dimly lit room. 'I don't know what you think is going on with me . . . but I lost my virginity to a girl I dated all through junior high. Before I even came to Waverly. It was only once, before we both left for school. It was just one of those things—'

Tinsley shook off Julian's hand. Hearing about Julian's past made her feel vaguely sick. But it wasn't Jenny he'd slept with? Why was she so obsessed with Jenny, anyway? She took a deep breath. 'Spare me the details, okay?'

A hurt look crossed Julian's face. He shuffled his feet and leaned against the wall. 'When I told you I wasn't a virgin, I kind of just wanted to sound cool, you know? You're older . . . and sometimes I get intimidated by you, despite how incredibly mature I am.' He shot her a shy smile, and Tinsley bit the inside of her cheek to keep from smiling back.

'That's true.' Tinsley tilted her head and fingered her silver and lime green dangling art deco earring. So . . . he'd had sex with a junior high girlfriend? That was barely a step above masturbation. 'I *am* very intimidating.'

'You have no fucking idea.' Julian shook his head, his eyes running up and down Tinsley's body. She shivered. 'But then I talked to Heath. And he told me you hadn't, well, done it . . . and I figured that was why you got so upset.'

Tinsley felt her face flushing – had she really made such

a big deal out of this? It didn't matter who Julian had been with before. That was in the past. Right now, he was looking at her in a way that made her forget everything else. She hopped up on the dryer and crossed her legs at the knee, letting the heels of her emerald green Christian Louboutin pumps clink against the metal side of the machine. 'Yeah?' she asked coolly. So maybe she could get over this. But it didn't mean she couldn't still tease him.

'Really.' Julian stepped toward her, placing a hand on her knee. It tickled, and totally turned her on. 'But I just don't really get why any of that's important. I want to be with you, and I think you want to be with me . . . despite that fake-pouty look on your face right now.'

Tinsley swatted his hand off her knee.

Julian grinned and planted his hands on top of the dryer, on either side of her. 'And we can wait. Until both of us are ready.'

Tinsley resisted the urge to grab his face and plant a wet kiss on his fine lips. The words *I want to be with you* rang in her ears. Suddenly, here in the Cambridge House laundry room, surrounded by boxes of Tide and shelves of cleaning supplies, Tinsley felt that all was right with the world.

Her almost black hair slid in front of her face like a curtain, and she cracked a devious smile. He'd done it just *once*? Everyone knew the first time was always terrible – a lot of fumbling around and trying to find stuff. It totally didn't count. Besides, junior high sex? Like *anyone* in junior high knew *anything*. Relief bubbled up in Tinsley's chest, and she nudged Julian's leg with the toe of her pump. 'I bet I could still teach you a few things.'

The expression on Julian's face relaxed and he threw his head back and laughed. 'I have no doubt about that.'

And neither did she.

27

IN TIMES OF DISTRESS, A WAVERLY OWL CAN
COUNT ON HIS ROOMMATE.

Brandon watched in disgust as Sage Francis, looking sleazy in a red dress about as big as a tissue, licked Lon Baruzza's neck and sprinkled salt on it. Incredibly unsanitary, Brandon thought, since Benny Cunningham had done a tequila shot off the exact same spot five minutes ago. Sage licked the salt off Lon's neck and swallowed the tequila, holding the back of Lon's head as she fished the lime from between his lips with her tongue. The crowd in the living room erupted in cheers.

Brandon tilted his head back, draining the last of his Hell Fire. The sweet syrup landed in his empty stomach with a thud and he felt for a moment like he might puke. He pushed his way into the kitchen and grabbed a water-stained glass from a kitchen cupboard. He filled it with water from the tap and took a long swig. Feeling suddenly alone, he longed for Hellie more than ever. Everyone was acting crazy. Jenny was like some kind of stranger, always walking around with a camera crew following her – although Brandon felt bad that those ungrateful frosh had made an embarrassing video of her. Callie was busy chasing after her new boyfriend. All his guy friends had been even bigger meatheads than usual recently, and after he'd orchestrated the whole Secret Satan mess, Heath was even more full of himself than usual.

Brandon sighed as Heath himself appeared in the kitchen doorway. He was still wearing his lame green suspenders and the Santa hat, although now his white T-shirt was covered with smudges of varying shades of red and pink, clearly left by eager female lips. A pair of girls' sunglasses was perched on his nose. 'What up?'

Brandon shrugged and stared at the dirty-cup-covered linoleum table. 'You give up asking everyone to sit on your lap and tell you what they want for Christmas?'

'Had to take a break. My lap hurts.' Heath set one of his full cups on the yellow kitchen counter, already sticky with spilled punch. 'Great party, huh?' He beamed proudly. 'Another success.' He held a cup in the air, toasting himself.

'Yeah, you can add it to your fucking résumé,' Brandon said, his voice dripping with sarcasm. He leaned against the cold edge of the sink. Outside the fogged-up window, the night looked dark and windy.

Heath didn't notice. He let out a loud whinny and a

girl across the room echoed it. Heath glanced in Kara's direction, probably hoping it was her. Brandon had caught Heath staring at her when she was on the dance floor with Alison Quentin, her tight-fitting floral-print silk dress swishing around her knees.

'Duuuddde,' Heath said, drawing out the word as he slung an arm across Brandon's shoulders. His sweaty stench rose up to Brandon's nose. 'I'm sorry about that male stripper.'

Brandon nearly stopped breathing. He shoved Heath's arm off, fighting the urge to twist it behind Heath's back and break it in two. Or maybe he should grab one of the black pots hanging over the food-crusted stove and smash it into Heath's smug, grinning face? 'I *knew* it was you.'

Heath raised his eyes to heaven and drunkenly made the sign of the cross. 'And I feel very, very bad about it.'

'What about . . . all that other shit?' Brandon asked, too furious to actually say the words *male pole-dancer alarm clock* and *sperm piggy bank* out loud.

Heath held up both hands, spilling a little Hell Fire on his fuzzy red pants. They made him look more like Elmo than Santa Claus. 'Guilty as charged.' He took a long swallow, finishing his first cup, which he dropped to the floor. 'I kept all the stuff from your real Secret Satan,' he added.

'You're fucking kidding me.' Brandon clenched his hands into fists.

'Lame stuff. Some kind of plaid scarf – right up your

alley.' Heath picked up his second cup. 'But I'm keeping the *Fletch* DVD,' he continued. 'It's a classic.'

'You're a dick,' Brandon said flatly. He'd always half-hated Heath, but he'd never expected Heath to go so far out of his way to make someone miserable.

'Dude, I just had to be sure.' Heath shrugged and snapped his suspenders. 'It was kind of a test. To know once and for all that you weren't, you know . . .'

Brandon grabbed a black frying pan from the rack and held it like a baseball bat.

'Kidding, kidding!' Heath held up his hands in self-defense. 'God, relax. It's a party. I said I was sorry, didn't I?'

Brandon knew he was lucky to get that much contrition from Heath, but something made him blurt out exactly what he was thinking. 'You sure you didn't do all this because I hooked up with Helga and you struck out with Gretchen?' The morning after Thanksgiving, when he and Heath had walked home from Dunderdorf's house, Heath had admitted that despite Gretchen's hotness, he hadn't sealed the deal. It felt good to stick this verbal knife in Heath's gut and turn it. He was prepared for Heath to deny it and move on, taking his stupid silly grin with him, but to his surprise a frown spread across Heath's face.

'Fuck you! I could have totally had her if I wanted.' He drank half his second cup and wiped his mouth with the back of his hand, his eyes still scanning the party, probably looking for Kara. 'Fuck you,' he said again, a little weakly.

Brandon barely had time to gloat before Heath slapped him on the shoulder.

'Dude, before I change my mind, here's your real present – straight from Santa Claus.' Heath reached into the back pocket of his ridiculous pants. Brandon was expecting another packet of synthetic sperm, like the one he'd found in his mailbox this morning. But instead Heath handed him a long envelope. He turned it over in his hand.

'What? Coupons to the gay bar in Poughkeepsie? You shouldn't have,' Brandon said sarcastically. He opened the envelope, surprised to find a voucher for an airline ticket to Switzerland in his name.

He looked at Heath, unsure of what to say. Heath Ferro? Going out of his way to buy his roommate an expensive airline ticket? So that he could visit his Swiss girlfriend? That was actually . . . really nice.

'Have a good time, buddy,' Heath said, slapping him on the shoulder again. A devious grin spread across his face. 'Thought you could use some holiday cheer, after all my hazing. Bring me back some chocolate or something.'

Brandon struggled to find the words. 'Thanks, dude.' He coughed into his fist.

'You can thank me by getting laid and shutting up about it.' Just then, a couple of squealing senior girls grabbed Heath by the suspenders and dragged him away.

'Come on, Santa,' Evelyn Dahlie cooed, grabbing Heath's hat and sliding it onto her bleached blond head. Brandon watched as Heath swung his arms around the girls. So Heath wasn't such a bad roommate/friend/person after all. He'd have to think about that more later.

For now, all he could think about was showing Hellie how much he missed her.

28

A WISE OWL KNOWS WHEN TO KISS AND
MAKE UP.

'You look really sexy tonight, by the way,' Sebastian whispered into Brett's ear as they stood on the dark porch of Cambridge House. 'With your hair up like that.' He touched his fingers gently to the back of Brett's neck, and she shivered, though not from the cold outside. That, she barely noticed.

'Thanks,' she murmured, enjoying the touch of his other hand against the small of her back. She could practically feel the heat coming through her black-and-white checkered Betsey Johnson coat.

Part of her was tempted to pull Sebastian into the backseat of his Mustang and spend a few hours steaming up the windows. Sebastian had spent the walk over from the Prescott Club holding Brett's hand and casually convincing her that the failed Holiday Ball wasn't her fault. Already she felt a teensy bit better about the whole thing.

But she knew there was something she had to do first, even though the last place she wanted to go was inside the party. 'I've got to find Callie.'

Sebastian sighed heavily and ran his hand over his hair. 'I should talk to her too.'

As soon as she opened the door, Brett was hit with a warm whoosh of beer-and-cigarette-scented air. So *this* was where everyone was. The living room was a pulsing dance floor, bodies pressed against one another in the tinted red light. Kind of tacky, Brett thought with a wave of bitterness, eyeing the floor-to-ceiling bookcases covered with red cellophane – her Holiday Ball decorations had been way better than this. Especially these gross lip-shaped mistletoes. But people were laughing and hugging each other as they found their Secret Satans, and she had to admit, they looked like they were having a lot more fun than they would have had with Dean Marymount and the stuffy Waverly alums breathing down their necks.

Everyone's eyes turned toward her and Sebastian. Her classmates all had sheepish grins on their faces, as if embarrassed for her. But Brett took a deep breath, stuck her chin in the air, and handed Sebastian her coat to hang on the overflowing coatrack. She wasn't about to let anyone feel bad for her because of the lame party. What the fuck did she care, anyway? She smiled smugly at the faces that turned to see her.

'Busted!' Heath yelled from where he was sitting in a high-backed leather armchair, a Santa hat tilted rakishly on his tousled blond head. 'How was your party, captain?'

Brett smiled sweetly at him and flipped a plum-manicured middle finger in his direction.

'Glad you could make it!' He winked as some senior girl with her hair in pigtails sat down on his lap. 'Tell me what Santa can bring you for Christmas, baby,' he cooed at the girl.

Brett spied a familiar pink satin dress with puffy tulle skirt over by the stereo. 'Hey,' she said, touching Sebastian's arm. 'Could you get me a drink?'

Sebastian looked up and saw Callie, then turned his eyes back to Brett. 'I should go apologize to her, too, I guess.'

'No,' Brett replied, squeezing his hand. 'Let me.' She cut through the crowd and approached her friend, who was staring at the rows of bookshelves as if memorizing the titles. From the rigid way she was holding her neck, she had clearly already seen Brett and Sebastian enter together.

Brett took a deep breath. 'Please don't be mad.' She raised her voice to be heard over the sound of a Dandy Warhols song.

Callie planted a hand on her hip and narrowed her eyes at Brett. Her lips were pressed together tightly. 'Don't be *mad*? You stole my *boyfriend*.' Her voice was tinged with bitterness.

Brett did feel guilty about kissing Sebastian, but . . . 'I wouldn't have kissed him if I thought you were serious about him,' she said honestly, twisting her watch nervously. 'You weren't, were you?'

Callie paused. 'He was a bit of a work-in-progress,' she answered petulantly, running her fingers over the iPod stereo. 'But that doesn't mean it feels good to have him taken away.'

'But he was a project to you, not a *person*. And that's not fair.' Brett placed her hand on Callie's thin forearm and squeezed it gently. 'You liked the person you thought he could be if you got rid of his Bon Jovi. And bad cologne.'

Callie considered this, glancing away while chewing the corner of her lip. 'He has terrible taste in music.'

'I know.' Brett grinned goofily, just thinking about the ride home from New Jersey with Sebastian, when they both sang along to the lame lyrics of 'I'll Be There for You'. 'But I like him despite the bad taste. Or maybe because of it. I don't know.'

Callie twitched her nose and arched her well-plucked eyebrows. 'That's impressive.'

'I know.' Brett laughed. 'And don't take this the wrong way, but I kind of think you were . . . just looking for someone to help you get over Easy.'

Callie sighed. Brett was right. Callie hadn't really been interested in Sebastian at all. She just liked the idea of having someone to keep her mind off Easy. As her eyes strayed briefly from Brett's face, she caught the gaze of Parker Dubois's pretty blue-gray eyes from across the room, and a surge of electricity shot through her. That definitely wasn't a look a gay guy gives a girl.

Suddenly Callie remembered why she'd broken up with
Easy. Because she wasn't ready to be with the love of her
life. Not yet, at least. Not when she was so young, and
there were still so many boys to kiss. Ones who looked like
Parker Dubois.

Finally, she dragged her eyes back to Brett and gave her
a sheepish grin. 'I guess you're right.'

'Right about what?' Tinsley asked, sidling up next to
them.

Brett looked at Callie and threw an arm around her
shoulder. 'Right about needing another drink.' Callie
giggled.

'I'll get it.' Brett caught Sebastian's eye in the drink line
and held up two fingers. 'You want one?' she asked Tinsley.

'Julian's getting me one.' Tinsley shrugged and tugged
at the top of her sunshine yellow dress, which was sliding
down a little. 'But thanks.'

'What are we going to drink to?' Brett asked, watching
Benny Cunningham try to flirt with Sebastian as he poured
a couple cups of punch. He smiled politely at her before
turning back to Brett and winking.

'How about . . . starting over?' Tinsley asked, flashing
another smile at Brett. Brett just stared at her. They'd been
civil to each lately, sure . . . but was Tinsley actually saying
she wanted to be friends again? Real friends?

'Did you just get high or something?' Callie asked,
pressing the back of her hand to Tinsley's forehead.

Tinsley rolled her eyes. 'No. I'm just saying . . . it's

practically a new year, turning over a new leaf, et cetera, et cetera.' She made a 'blah, blah, blah' motion with her hand.

'I think she's high on Juuuuulian,' Brett teased, kicking away an empty plastic cup that had rolled into her foot.

'Fuck you,' Tinsley shot back, but it was one of those friendly fuck-yous that you can only say to people you love. All the skirmishes of the past four months flashed through Brett's mind, but she realized that none of them mattered as much as having Tinsley's friendship back. She could be a manipulative bitch, sure – but that was what made her so much fun.

Sebastian strode up balancing three cups of Hell Fire in his hands. Brett and Callie each grabbed one. Sebastian glanced at both girls, relief registering on his handsome face when he realized they'd made up. 'Cheers,' Brett cried, holding up her glass and planting a big kiss on Callie's cheek.

'Knock it off.' Callie shoved Brett away affectionately. 'I've got work to do.'

'Those girls suck,' Tinsley proclaimed, watching a couple of sophomores fall off from their perch on the coffee table. 'Come on.' She grabbed Brett and Callie by the hands and jumped up on the hand-carved coffee table as catcalls went up around the room. Sebastian cranked the volume as the girls danced, holding their cups over their heads.

Callie could feel the music moving through her as she gyrated above the crowd, all eyes on her. She flashed a smile at Tinsley, who turned and smiled down at Julian. She caught

Brett winking at Sebastian, who gave a hearty thumbs-up from the back of the room. She wished she had someone to smile at, or throw a wink at . . . but then she realized that at least half a dozen guys – maybe more – were staring right at her.

It felt good to have fun again. Not fake fun, like she was trying to have with Sebastian. She finally admitted to herself that her last good time had been spent with Easy – she wasn't totally over him yet.

But she'd get there. She moved her body in time to the music that made the whole room vibrate, closing her eyes to feel it in her bones.

A WAVERLY OWL KNOWS THAT FAILURES ARE WHAT MAKE SUCCESS SO SWEET.

As the room spun around her, Jenny pushed through the crowd, desperately searching for her black wool Banana Republic peacoat. It wasn't where she left it, and she wasn't about to freeze her limbs off walking home without it. She must have picked up a dozen black peacoats only to discover that they belonged to someone else. She felt sweaty and humiliated – everywhere she turned, people were staring at their phones, giggling, or asking her really embarrassing questions, like *Can I see your bra again?* and *Where are your bunny pajamas?* All she wanted to do now was find her coat, slink to her room unseen, curl up under her baby-soft quilt, and never come out again.

Heath Ferro sat in a giant leather rocking chair in the corner. The line of girls waiting to sit in his lap and tell him what they wanted for Christmas had only a few drunken stragglers in it. 'J-bear!' he cried out, drunkenly, when Jenny brushed past him. 'Come ask Santa for a sexy negligee. Anything's better than those flannels you wear.'

Jenny rolled her eyes. She spotted the open door of a hall closet, and remembered Kaitlin offering to hang up her coat. She wasn't even mad at the freshman girls anymore. She deserved what they'd done to her after spending the last two weeks prancing around like she was the star of her own reality series. What had she been thinking? She didn't even *like* reality TV.

'Jenny Humphrey!' someone screeched. Even though the last thing she wanted was for someone else to tell her she looked terrible in the morning, Jenny couldn't help whirling around.

To her surprise, it was Tinsley Carmichael who'd called out to her. She stood on top of a coffee table, looking fabulously elegant in a canary yellow cocktail dress with a sweetheart neckline. On one side of her was Brett, her bright red hair looking dramatic against her pale skin and dark purple dress, and on the other, Callie, whose loose blond curls hung around her head, making her look like some kind of sun goddess. Jenny immediately thought of the Three Graces, the figures in Greek mythology who represented beauty, charm, and elegance.

Jenny felt her cheeks flush. All eyes were on her, or at least, it felt that way, and she swore the room got quieter as everyone strained to hear what Tinsley would say to her.

'What?' she asked shakily, kind of hoping it would be the
end of everything. Was Tinsley about to put the icing on
the cake and tell her she had no place at this school and
she might as well crawl back to loserdom – or join the
chess club or something? Brett and Callie were too good
for her, too. Jenny should have known better and stuck
with the dorky, safe people like Yvonne Stidder from the
very beginning.

Tinsley tossed her dark mane of hair over her shoulder.
Then she reached her hand down, a thick platinum cuff
sliding down her wrist. 'Get your cute little butt up here.'

Jenny just stood there, her cherry-ChapSticked mouth
slightly open. She felt like time had stopped, the way it
did in a nightmare – or a dream. Tinsley Carmichael, who'd
been a bitch to her all week, was inviting Jenny in front of
the whole world . . . to dance with the cool kids? Jenny's
feet felt like they were glued to the floor. She would have
stayed there, if Brett hadn't hopped down, her bare feet
landing gracefully on the carpet. She grabbed Jenny's wrist
and tugged her toward the table. Jenny could practically
feel the tears welling up in her eyes. 'I'm sorry I blew off
your party.'

'Whatever. It sucked.' Brett laughed, a carefree look in
her almond-shaped green eyes that Jenny hadn't seen in a
long time. 'But that means you have to make up for it now.'
She pushed Jenny toward the table, and Callie and Tinsley
moved aside to make room.

Jenny took a deep breath just as the first notes of the

AC/DC song 'You Shook Me All Night Long' came on. She felt eyes on her as she hopped up on the table with the three most glamorous girls in school. *Her friends*. Tinsley bumped her hip against hers, and Callie gave her a wink, as if to say, *Yeah, you looked like a total dork in that video but we still love ya*. Jenny's head whirled, and as she started to move her body to the music, the blood pulsing through her veins, she felt like a new person. Or maybe just the person she'd always been.

After all, who needed a fan club when you had great friends?

BennyCunningham: It was Cliff Montgomery who gave me my ferret. Think I should ask him out?

VerenaArneval: Sure. Gifts of rodents bode well for romance.

BennyCunningham: Who was your Satan? U find out?

VerenaArneval: Yvonne Stidder! She gave me penis-shaped lollipops!

BennyCunningham: Ew.

OwlNet Instant Message Inbox

HeathFerro: Sorry to hear your boyfriend likes redheads better than blondes! Need someone to lick your wounds?

CallieVernon: Gross! Don't you have some penis candy canes to eat?

HeathFerro: You're my Secret Satan? I KNEW you had a dirty side!!

CallieVernon: Don't get used to it.

AlisonQuentin: Guess who I saw in old lady Apthorp's office when I handed in my Chaucer paper? Her replacement. She's retiring over break!

EmilyJenkins: AFT. I think she wears Depends.

AlisonQuentin: Wait till you hear the good part. The guy replacing her has two kids that are transferring in. Saw the whole fam on my way out of her office.

EmilyJenkins: Ohmigod. Boys, I hope. We need some new blood.

AlisonQuentin: A boy and a girl. Both tall, well-dressed, dark hair with green eyes. And otherworldly hot.

EmilyJenkins: Happy New Year to Waverly!

Don't miss the delicious prequel to the bestselling
GOSSIP GIRL series.

the GOSSIP GIRL prequel
IT HAD TO BE YOU

Step into the world of the rich and fabulous

*Once upon a time on the Upper East Side of New York
City, two beautiful girls fell in love with one perfect boy . . .*

*If anyone is going to tell this story it has to be me. I know
everything, and what I don't know I'll invent, elaborately.*

You know you love me,

Gossip Girl

Welcome to the thrilling world of GOSSIP GIRL and
Manhattan's exclusive single-sex private schools,
inhabited by the city's beautiful elite; there's
jealousy, betrayal and outrageous behaviour.

IT HAD TO BE YOU goes back to the hot and sultry
summer when the love triangle started between
Blair Waldorf, Serena van der Woodsen and Nate
Archibald – and there's a lot more to this story than
anyone realises. Scandalous secrets are exposed and
you might find out just how the legendary GOSSIP
GIRL column began . . .